INTO THE LION'S MOUTH

NANCY MCCONNELL

Immortal Works LLC
1505 Glenrose Drive
Salt Lake City, Utah 84104
Tel: (385) 202-0116

© 2021 Nancy McConnell
www.nancymcconnell.com

Cover Art by Ashley Literski
http://strangedevotion.wixsite.com/strangedesigns

This book is a work of fiction. Names, characters, businesses, organizations, places, events and incidents either are the product of the author's imagination or are used fictitiously. Any resemblance to actual persons, living or dead, events, or locales is entirely coincidental.

ISBN 978-1-953491-24-4 (Paperback)
ASIN B09C4BXQB1 (Kindle Edition)

For Ross and Shirley Walker, exceptional parents
Thank you for teaching me the beauty of love

Author's Note

Whenever I read historical fiction, I always want to sort out which parts are real and which parts are invented, so for people like me, here is the breakdown.

The inspiration for this story came when I visited Venice with my family. While wandering through the Doge's Palace, I thought about the many wonderful tales that must have happened inside those walls. As a writer, I am always looking for stories, so when I got home, I started reading all I could about this fascinating and unique city. I fell in love with it all over again and wanted to share my passion with children around the world. The truth is Venice is really sinking and, if we don't do something, eventually we will lose this amazing treasure. I hope to inspire a new generation to love Venice, so together we might do what it takes to preserve this precious part of our past.

There were so many exciting things to write about, so at first, it was hard to know where to begin. But when I came across the custom of recruiting an orphan child to help with the election of a new doge, I knew I had my beginning.

While Nico rose from my imagination, some of the characters in the book did not. The Bellinis—Jacopo, Giovanni, and Gentile—were respected artists in Venice. Venice was renowned for its wonderful artwork, and the Bellini family produced some of its most treasured pieces. Being fortunate enough to live in a prosperous trade city, Venetian painters had access to the best quality paints and pigments, so their works became famous around the world because they were the most vibrant and colorful. Gentile was the official state painter for the doge; he painted the portrait of Doge Mocenigo, and he traveled to Constantinople to paint Sultan Mehmet II. His painting of the parade for the election of a new doge is one of his most important. You can find them online easily. I copied any physical descriptions of people and places I could from these paintings.

Queen Caterina Cornaro was also an actual person and the only woman to ever rule the island of Cyprus. She remained the ruler after her husband King James' death until the Venetian ruling council decided they needed a man to do the job. There was a bit of this kind of silly thinking back then. So they brought her home and sent a man to take her place, and the people were unhappy about it.

The orphan hospital did exist. Times were tough and often children who were not even orphans ended up there because their families could not care for them. There are many records of children left there for a time and later picked up when their families' situations improved. Although Lisabetta's character is fictional, I took her name from one child who spent time there. Her parents wrote a sad letter to the nurses asking them to take special care of their daughter. Since there was no way to know what happened to the real Lisabetta, I wanted to give her a happy ending, so I added her to the story.

And now a word about the origins of Lord Newcastle. In my research I came across the most interesting of Venetians. His name was Giacomo Casanova. A noted adventurer, Casanova was notorious throughout the world for his antics, unlawful activities, and affairs with married ladies. Since he lived about two hundred years after the time of this story, and since his actions were not at all wholesome, I did not think I could use the character as he appeared in history. But his adventurous escape from the Leads was too good to pass up. So I gave him a new name and country of origin and popped him right into the book. That's the fun of being a writer. There really are no rules. The real Casanova was, in fact, the only one to ever escape from the infamous Leads prison just as Newcastle and Nico do in the book. And if you haven't guessed already, Newcastle is my English version of Casanova (casa: castle; nova: new).

Other characters, like Stefano, Nurse Francesca, and Horatio, are products of my imagination, as are Captain Zeno and Lord Foscari. There was a real Lord Foscari on the doge's council, but he may have been a perfectly nice man; I merely took his name for my invented character. The Zeno family was prominent in Venice, and had captains, traders, and heroes as members.

It was a turbulent time in history, and Venice was caught between two empires who both wanted to claim her, the east and the west. There was much intrigue, and many treaties were signed and broken. The Venetians really tried to have Sultan Mehmet assassinated more than twenty-four times, but they never succeeded.

One last note about Father Vincenzo. He is not a fictional character but a real priest who lived about five hundred years after the time of this story. He was neither famous nor important, except to those who loved him. And in the end, I think this is the best way to be.

CHAPTER 1

I was the only orphan, in Nurse Francesca's memory, returned twice. This fact often peppered our exchanges, and so the sting remained fresh.

"Your time here in Venice has become unproductive," she said, looming over me.

She was a tall woman, mistress of the hospital, and not to be trifled with. A table separated us. I sat. She stood.

Apprehension fermented like rotted meat in my stomach.

"There is a farmer in Padua who is looking for a boy of your skills—which, quite frankly, are none—to pick olives. He will provide room and board for your labor."

I jumped up from my chair and grasped the edge of the table. Leave Venice? An unthinkable idea. "But—"

"Sit down," she commanded. There was steel under her wimple.

Reluctantly, I obeyed.

"I cannot keep a boy who refuses to help himself. You have failed to succeed in two apprenticeships, for reasons I cannot begin to understand. We can no longer take advantage of the generosity of others regarding you. This is my decision."

This burned much worse than a whipping. I opened my

mouth to protest, but she leaned on the table and sliced me in two with one look.

"You leave next week."

There was no point in arguing; she would not change her mind.

But I would not go. I could not leave Venice any more than I could cut off my right hand.

THE *PIAZZA SAN MARCO* was glorious even in the rain. The *Basilico* dominated the square. The church's arched rooftop bubbled across the sky like waves rolling off the lagoon. And from over the arched doorway the golden winged lion looked down upon its domain, mouth open in silent tribute to the powerful city. Colorful saintly statues topped its pillars, eyes heavenward, hands outspread. The building lived deeply in the heart of every Venetian.

All this, I failed to notice. My damaged feelings, raw from my recent encounter with Nurse Francesca, remained foremost in my mind. Stubbornness grew in my heart like a boil on a beggar's neck. I needed a plan.

Despite a greyish drizzle, the square bustled with activity. Wealthy merchants and ladies scurried across the cobbled streets, busy with their own duties and responsibilities. I slipped my hand into my pocket. Empty. If I was to make anything of a plan to escape a life of olives, I must address this lack with haste.

I scanned the piazza for a likely candidate. And there he was. A priggish looking nitwit sauntered along like a proud ostrich, neck stretched high, wings flapping, boring the young woman who walked at his side. Her head swiveled frequently, no doubt searching for an escape.

Seeing a bulge in his outer coat flap, I moved in closer.

"My dear, you must really see Rome. The city is magnificent," the popinjay droned on at the poor lady. She nodded her head absently from time to time as her companion prattled on. I picked up a small white plume from the ground and approached the couple.

"Excuse me, milady, did this fall from your hat," I asked.

The two stopped, and the young woman peered closely at my offering. The corners of her mouth turned up and she studied the scruffy thing I held out, as if a dirty feather could be of importance to her.

"Of course not, you idiot," the prig snapped angrily. "Get that filthy thing away from us."

The lady smiled apologetically, and I dipped my head.

"So sorry to bother you," I said, stepping only slightly aside.

The boorish young dandy pushed past me, decrying such lowlife in the piazza, and apologizing to his companion for my filth. His coat brushed me as they moved by.

The weight of his modest purse landed deftly in my pocket and the couple walked on unaware. I melted into the crowd, then ducked behind one of the basilica's pillars to examine my prize. Unfortunately, hot air was the gentleman's biggest possession. The pouch contained only a copper coin of small value and some buttons and pebbles. I sighed. His attempt to look rich had worked on me, at any rate.

My eye caught the open door to the cathedral. Something tugged at me and drew me forward as a fly drawn to honey. I slipped inside.

In the darkened interior of the holy building, I made my way to the pew closest to the front. Kneeling, I crossed myself and bent my head. How bold of me to sit like this, asking for favors from God, when I had tested the patience of many living saints. My most recent activity gave witness to this. But I *was* bold.

My prayer was a simple one: to change my destiny. I belonged to Venice. My heart was sewn to this city with thread stronger than the ropes of a galley's sails. I was not a devout Venetian, but if my intention to remain was to succeed, it needed some spiritual weight. And so, under the bones of St. Mark himself, I stated my plan and hoped the words would reach the ears of God.

As I exited the church, I threw the dandy's single copper into the collection box. The money would do more good there than in my pocket. Pulling my thin cover over my head as protection from the rain, I moved into the open square. After barely taking two steps, someone wrapped their arms around my neck, yanking my jacket down over my eyes.

A yelp escaped my lips as I struggled. "Let me go," I shouted, but the coat muffled my shouts. Surely a small copper would not be my undoing.

A familiar chuckle, like that of a small chicken, sounded. My heart rate slowed. I needn't be fearful of that chuckle, but I increased my efforts to break away. Wrenching my arm free, I turned to my former captor.

"Stefano, you whelp," I hollered, attempting to wipe the grin off his face with a well-placed punch to the jaw. He easily held me at arm's length and thumped me soundly—but not severely—a few more times. He had several pounds on me, and it was little use struggling to defend myself against his onslaught.

"That," he said, out of breath, "was for making me tell lies to Nurse Francesca about where you were." He grinned broadly, victory showing plainly on his slim face.

"I never asked you to lie," I retorted, straightening my shirt, and discovering another rip.

A group of younger boys surrounded Stefano. They were dressed like us, in plain shirts and pants a trifle too short, signaling them as younger members of our unofficial order of orphans. The smallest of the three, Antonio, was often under our feet at the *Ospedale della Pietà*, our orphan home. He'd received a cuff or two from Stefano on occasion but that had not dulled his devotion. He stared up at us, mouth slightly open, head tilted to the side like a dog surveying its beloved master. The older two were less devout, but still jockeyed for the closest position to us, brows furrowed and eyes wide. Ready to offer an opinion to their better if it were required of them. Stefano and I had worked hard to cultivate an impression of important worldliness among the younger residents of the orphanage. This was mainly to satisfy our own self-importance.

"What choice did I have? I couldn't tell her you were picking pockets in the piazza, could I? And if I didn't say something, she would harp on me like a pigeon at a puddle until she bloodied my ears with her words."

"You ripped my shirt."

"It's an improvement." He laughed. "What did Nurse want with you, anyway?"

I advised him of her edict and my impending departure from Venice. He whistled low and slow. "I can't see you in an olive orchard."

"Nor shall you," I responded.

"Was that you coming out of the basilica?" he asked, deciding it was time to change the subject. His lopsided grin told me his principal goal was to embarrass me. I did not take the bait.

"I had business to attend," I answered. The younger lads' eyes widened in astonishment. My bid to impress was successful.

Stefano grunted. "Bothering the Holy Father again?" He rolled his eyes skyward. "You will never be handsome, Nico, just give up."

"You're right," I responded, shaking my head in mock sadness. "From now on, I'll devote my prayers to asking Him to grant you the brain you so sadly lack."

A shadow fell across our group, interrupting our sparring.

"Child, I have need of you." A man in a black cloak clamped his hand tightly on the shoulder of Antonio, the youngest boy standing with us.

Antonio's eyes widened and his face filled with fear. The man's clothes and bearing indicated noble status. It was always best not to be noticed by your betters.

"I would be happy to help you, good sir." I spoke up somewhat out of pity, for the lad's distress was obvious, and because rendering a service to someone of this man's stature might serve me well. Mayhap this was the opportunity I needed to stay my expulsion from my beloved city. The Lord worked fast. I did not know then how those words sealed my fate to a far worse one than olives.

The man's eyes were deep, like black pits in his face, and his mouth turned up slightly at the corners. He redirected his attention when I spoke, and his powerful gaze came to rest upon me.

"Hmm," he grunted. "And what does this boy think, I wonder?" Antonio let out a breath, although his body remained frozen. The fellow dropped his hand. "The task I have requires little wit, but since you have so eagerly volunteered, I accept your offer. Tell me, can you keep your mouth shut?"

I nodded my head, raising one eyebrow. He narrowed his pit-like eyes and stroked his greying beard, surveying me. The force of his look was strong, and had he held me in it a moment longer, I might have looked away.

"Come." The bearded interloper pivoted. His cloak, flying out behind him, sent drops of rain like holy water on my small band of confederates.

I followed. The decision was either the most foolish, or the wisest, I had ever made. My mind raced as we crossed the piazza. The day was wet, and my shoes sank into one of the many murky puddles gathering in the square. As usual, the sea asserted her dominance over the city.

The cobblestones were uneven, and water collected in enormous pools difficult to avoid. I was accustomed to soggy feet, but I wondered at this man's lack of concern for his expensive leather boots. My first apprenticeship to a cobbler did not last long; I could not hide my obvious revulsion at the daily putrid parade of feet. But in time, I learned the value of good footwear.

My companion walked with swift strides towards the *Palazzo Ducale*–the heart of Venice. As we hurried, I wondered at the man's occupation. He did not look like a carpenter (my second attempt at apprenticeship) or a cobbler. Perhaps he was a wealthy merchant. His clothes and bearing spoke of authority. My prospects were already looking up. I wiped rain across my face, hoping to clear away any grime accumulated there since last I washed. With no reflection to peer into, I had no idea if I was successful or not.

With the weather came fog. Under such a heavy, grey blanket the activity on the nearby lagoon was hidden, but the sound of oars splashing through the water meant, despite the dampness, business continued. We passed only a few yards from the water's edge, where gondolas carrying people and goods would arrive and depart the piazza. The smell of rotting wood and mold gave way to the cleansing saltiness of sea air. Venice lived and breathed her nautical history.

My limbs quivered. I was never unaffected by the life of the city. There was an imperceptible bond tying me to her—to her merchants and seafarers, to her nobles and paupers, to her artists and priests. This city was the only mother I had ever known.

We veered left towards the palace, the home of our ruler, the doge, a man chosen from the finest citizens to set a course for the city. The building stretched along the *Molo*, Venice's most famous waterfront street. Its columned facade was the impressive view greeting new arrivals to Venice. I envied those witnessing the splendor for the first time.

As we drew closer my scalp tingled. I'd never crossed that ornate threshold. My ears burned as blood rushed to my head, sending shivers of joy pulsing in my throat. I often dreamed of walking through these doors as a respected member of the council. In Venice, even an orphan could rise to high government. Still, I was not there yet. I kept as close as possible to my companion, fearing a rebuke followed by a cuff from a passing guard might end my chances of realizing a dream.

"Where are your parents?" he asked as we walked.

"I have none."

"The great sickness?"

"Yes."

It was not necessary to explain further. An orphan of the plague was as commonplace as a fish in a net. Both my father and mother died before I could walk. This was a source of great bitterness to me. At least one of them should have cared enough about my future to have attempted to live.

We ascended the few steps to the entrance. The guard, in his stiff collar and un-Venetian red cloak, moved aside after a brief word from my benefactor. This is how I now thought of him, for he must be a man of wealth and power to enter this place so freely.

"The election of a new doge is upon us."

I nodded. This was common knowledge. In Venice, politics were a matter of concern for all. Our elections were the pride of the Serene Republic for, in all the world, we alone elected our leaders. No despotic kings or emperors for our city.

"You are about to become part of a noble tradition, lad."

The spasm in my throat increased and I could barely croak out a response. "I am?"

"Yes. Just do as you are told, and all will be well," he answered.

The beauty of the palazzo was enough to make dreams come to life. To say the palace was like a treasure was to say a man and a pig were equals. Works of great art, illuminating the vibrant past of the Venetian Republic, graced every surface. Ancient heroes looked down upon me, urging me on to victory. Their arms raised, swords drawn, both encouraged and humbled me as my eyes raked the ornately painted ceilings and walls cocooning us. I recognized the blind Doge Enrico Dandolo, as he set forth on his Holy Crusade. I put my hand to my cheek, half expecting to feel it moist from the spray of salt water.

We entered a room much larger than those we had previously passed through.

"This is the *Sala Maggiore*, the meeting place of the Great Council," my guide said. "Gathered here are four hundred of the noblest in Venice, those who hold the destiny of the city in their hands and so, consequently, yours as well."

In the crowded room, my ears became full of the dull roar of hundreds of men all talking at once. I gulped. It was easy to feign confidence among my fellow orphans, but here, in this group of illustrious Venetians, my palms moistened and my legs quaked. Guilt associated with my past deeds welled up inside of me. I studied the faces around me, hoping there were none whose pockets I might have raided.

A firm hand on my neck made me jump. My companion

urged me on, and I pressed down on my jangled nerves as we went forward.

In the center of the room, surrounded by a formidable crowd of well-dressed gentlemen, a craggy-faced man bellowed, "Fellow Venetians, it is time to exercise our right as members of this Most Serene Republic to choose our next doge. You represent the most noble, the worthiest, and distinguished families in the city. Some have been here since the first gondola paddled into these swampy waters to escape bloodthirsty Huns. The sacrifices of our forefathers have made it possible for us to live in the greatest city in Christendom."

A cheer rose from the crowd, and I joined with the people in feather caps and thick hose, as together we swelled with pride at the accomplishments of our wonderful ancestors.

"Today we choose not only for ourselves, but for all Venetians, from the wealthiest merchant to the poorest orphan." He motioned to my guardian, who pushed me forward. Fear paralyzed me. My companion shoved harder, and in my stunned state, I lost my balance. Sturdy arms, whose owner I knew not, caught me before I fell and spun me to face the crowd.

"As tradition dictates, we have here a lad, which excellent Captain Zeno has brought from the streets, a symbol of unity among all Venetians." A tug of disappointment damped my growing hope as I learned my benefactor's identity. He was a seafarer; I would not find an apprenticeship at his side. There was no desire in me to sail to other lands. What would I discover not already here, at the crossroads of the world?

"This boy will distribute to each member of this Great Council a wax ball. If you find a piece of parchment inside, I charge you with the solemn duty of joining in our Council of Ten and selecting our next doge—a sacred trust afforded to those the Lord finds worthy. Let the selection begin. May God grant us wisdom."

Captain Zeno steered me towards a large urn filled with balls no bigger than grapes. "As each member approaches," he whispered in my ear, "give him one."

A line formed in front of me. Reaching into the ornate vessel, the sticky gobs stuck to the tips of my fingers. Fumbling, I brought out the first. A haughty nobleman dressed in a tight bodice and puffed sleeves stood before me, hand outstretched. A nudge in my side caused me to drop the ball into his palm. The man pulled open the lump; inside was a small piece of parchment. He held his prize up high.

"The choosing has begun," Captain Zeno called out.

Another councilor replaced the first. He dug into his ball and discovered only wax. Most found nothing, but as time moved on, a small group of finders began to gather to the side of the room.

Initially, I was delighted. Perhaps this was a chance for me to find favor with an important personage to the city. Maybe I would discover my own apprenticeship here in this room. But my delight soon waned as noble after noble barely cast an eye on me. I was as invisible as a foul odor. My brain whirled as I tried to think of some way to favorably impress this group, but no obvious avenues presented themselves to me.

I grew weary of the tedious job, but in time the urn emptied. I was eager not to lose the opportunity slipping away with each wax ball I handed out.

Soon the onlookers bored with the performance. They clustered in small groups, talking, paying little attention to the proceedings. And thus, of course, to me. The line grew shorter; my chance for advancement dwindled and disappointment seeped into my soul. It was a cruel trick to remain unseen in this illustrious company, yet I was helpless to change this likely outcome.

As I pondered my options, a pointy-bearded nobleman came to a stop in front of me. His black eyes bored into me, and he wore an expression somewhere between a sneer and a smile as he reached towards me.

I placed the ball into his open palm, an action I had now done already several hundred times. As my fingers released the item to his care, his palm tilted, and the ball fell to the floor.

"The fool has dropped it!" he exclaimed, glaring at me. His rather large foot twitched and came down squarely on top of the sticky dropped item. He bent as if to retrieve it. "A lively one, here it is!" he called out, holding up a ball.

Some members of the crowd tittered slightly at the performance, but then returned to their conversations.

"Lord Foscari, have you results?" Captain Zeno inquired.

"To be sure, it was worth it," Foscari said. In his grasp, he held a piece of parchment.

Our eyes met. Mine, full of astonishment. His, cold and hard. We both knew the ball he held up to the crowd was not the one I had given him, which was at this moment securely stuck to the bottom of his boot.

The man was a cheat.

I opened my mouth to protest, but the words would not come.

He turned from me and joined the growing group of chosen, moving awkwardly with the slight limp of someone whose footwear caused them grief. When he came to a stop before the fire, he set his booted foot on the edge of the hearth. I lifted my eyes from the boot. His gaze was still upon me.

Finally, I had the attention I'd wanted. But the heat from his glare made me wish I didn't.

CHAPTER
2

Only a few balls remained at the bottom of the jar. One of them still contained its prize, but with the Council of Ten now formed, a nearby attendant swept them up and threw them in the fire.

Captain Zeno steered me through the crowd to the front door. He pressed a coin into my hand and gave me a gentle push out. "You have done your duty as a Venetian today. Now, go tell your friends you helped to choose the new doge." He turned to leave, and I almost let him. I almost kept silent.

Almost.

"Captain Zeno?"

He raised an eyebrow at my daring. "You have something to say?"

"The man who dropped his wax ball, Lord Foscari."

"Yes, what about him?"

"I think, well, I think he switched it."

Zeno stroked his beard, those black pits again boring into me.

I rubbed my thumb over my chin echoing his movement. This was a recent affectation I had adopted in the hopes it made me look studious. In reality, I searched for any sharp or bristled hairs. Nurse Francesca insisted I had not yet reached my thirteenth year, but I was certain she was in error and manhood was close upon me. The skin remained obstinately smooth. Lowering my hand, I went on. "He dropped the wax on purpose, and then he stepped on it. He must have hand another in his pocket."

"You saw this?"

"Yes."

"Does he know?"

"Yes."

Zeno closed his eyes and grimaced. "You have made a dangerous enemy today. Forget it, and you may yet live."

"But he's a cheat, a man of a character not worthy to be in such a great company," I persisted.

"If a noble spirit were a requirement of our rulers, there would be an empty palazzo in San Marco."

I folded my arms across my chest and gave him a hard stare. He had the grace to chuckle ruefully.

"Fear not, there are considerable men of worth within our hallowed walls of government. Don't worry over much about Foscari; he will be only one of ten to choose our next candidates for doge. However"—his voice grew more serious— "I suggest you not put yourself in his sight again too soon. He would not like to think a lad of your status sat in judgment of him. Are you without faults you would keep concealed?"

My face flushed and hot words rose to my lips. What was the petty thieving of an orphan compared to the cheating of our government? There was no chance to reply because with this assertion, he put our conversation to an end and vanished back inside the building. I clenched my hand, surprised to discover something hard in my palm. It was the coin he had given me, a *soldo*. An honestly gained one. It was solid between my fingers. One side was flat where someone had clipped away some of the precious metal. Still, the damage was small. Good had come of my misadventure, despite the captain's ominous warning. I had not found my apprenticeship, but perhaps this would be the beginning of my fortune.

I pocketed the coin and ran across the piazza through the archway leading to the *Calle Dei Mercuria* and towards *Campo San Zulian*. Vendors crowded the pavement. Shopkeepers spilled out from their shops, hoping to snare a few more customers. Only a nimble frame could maneuver with any speed through the swarming throng. I received a few swats from annoyed merchants or patrons as I snaked my way through the packed street. My destination in sight, *Eglise San Zulian*, I made one last swerving jog and mounted the steps to the building. Inside the church, I removed my hood.

"Father Vincenzo," I called, turning my head and straining my eyes in the dimness, attempting to spot the curate.

The priest was arranging the altar, his usual station. Today he polished the nobbled silver candlesticks as lovingly as if they were the Savior's own feet. I ran down the middle aisle and, remembering where I was, stopped by the stairs, genuflected, and crossed myself.

The old man, his task complete, descended the steps to join me. In the dim church light, I could make out his stern face. "Nico, I have not seen you at mass for weeks."

"Forgive me, Father," I said, averting my gaze, "but God has not been far from my heart."

We sat together in the pew and he listened to the account of my recent adventure without comment, his grey head nodding and his bushy eyebrows dancing up and down on his forehead as my tale unfolded. I did not mention Foscari. The incident was best forgotten.

"So," he said at the end of my story, "you have come now

to share your newfound wealth with the Lord?" No smile curled his lips, but the little darts at the corners of his eyes deepened.

"Not exactly, Father." I squirmed. "I hoped you might bless this coin so it would increase. Then I would be in a much better position to participate in God's work."

The priest threw his head back and laughed. "Nico, you are a true Venetian, piety and business all in one. Let us bless your earnings today and see what destiny our Savior will visit upon you. But, there is a condition."

"Yes, Father?"

"You must take yourself in hand, Nico. Nurse Francesca tells me you have not treated your latest apprenticeships with any gravity. I hope this is the first of many more fairly-gained coins in your possession."

"It was *shoes*," I scoffed, kicking at the leg of the pew in front of me. I deliberately ignored the emphasis he put on *fairly earned*. He suspected, occasionally, that I got a small penny or two without the knowledge of the giver. He scolded me more than once on this subject, but it had not turned him against me. For some reason, my mother's sake perhaps, the good priest accepted responsibility for my eternal soul, and he was not one to give up on such a grave task.

"Nonetheless, Nico, a boy in your situation cannot afford to look down upon honest work."

The accusation stung me, for I was honest in my dealings with those who truly mattered to me.

"But Father, to leave Venice and pick olives? Do you genuinely think the Lord is calling me to this?" I had no intention of repeating this conversation. I had heard often from my elders about my need to take life seriously, and to pay attention to my responsibilities, and to keep my hands to myself. The best course of action was to put on a sorrowful face and slump my shoulders forward in apparent remorse. "If it is the Lord's desire, I suppose I could grow to like olives."

"Don't assume I am fooled by your acting," the good cleric said, his voice stern. "Nico, play the fool too long and you will find you are one."

"Father, you need not worry about me, especially now my fortune has begun. I promise to consider what you have said, but will you not bless the beginning of this poor orphan's new destiny?" I held up the piece once again.

He shook his head but agreed, solemnly sprinkling holy water on the coin and me. He prayed we would prosper the Lord's work in the realm. "And Lord, teach this boy to be sober and responsible. Amen."

I silently disavowed this last part. Sober responsibility was not how I planned to succeed. Wit and ambition were my talents.

I bade goodbye to the priest and headed for the center of the *campo* to weigh my dining options. A soldo could buy several excellent meals, but this one was special. A blessed coin would be good seed for my future fortune. A careful purchase could be the door to my new destiny.

There would be a hot meal at the Pietá. The Most Serene Republic of Venice, being a city of civilized and devoted citizens, regarded it as a pious duty to house widows and orphans. The care was excellent, but I preferred making my own way in the world.

I surveyed the pockets and purses of the surrounding crowds. My skill at finding the most likely prospects was excellent, and I was well acquainted with the most lucrative areas of the campo.

I knew the city well, having explored it since I was a wee tot still messing my pants. In those days, I frequently slipped from the concerned care of the sisters. Not for thievery, mind, just to uncover the mysteries of the twisting and turning corridors of this wondrous place, unencumbered by the supervisory eye of my elders. The Lord must have sent a lesser angel to watch over me, for I came to no harm, despite Nurse Francesca's constant fear of my drowning in a canal. But I wouldn't drown. I was a child of Venice; my veins ran with sea water and salt. If I tumbled into the murky canals, the mother Adriatic would only have spat me back on shore, a wet fish swatting my behind for my impudence.

These thoughts were interrupted by a rough tug on my shirt. I stumbled into the angry form of a nasty looking bruiser, his hand clenched firmly on my collar.

"You, boy, come with me. Quietly," he said, leaning in close. The noxious, alcohol-scented breath assailed my nose. "Lord Foscari wants to speak with you."

My body went cold. In an encounter with this sort of villain, even Mother Venice's protection would not save me from a watery grave. Wrenching free, I ran. Heavy footsteps clattered behind me and harsh voices called out.

My long days of wandering about the city allowed me a clear advantage. I knew the streets as a monk knows his Bible. With speed increased by the wings of fear, I turned down one street, then the next. The rhythm of running feet was loud and staccato, but in the tight echoing passageways, it was impossible to tell how close the chaser grew. Indeed, the echoes sounded as if a small army was after me.

Ahead, a modest bridge arced over the *Riva della Fava*, a busy canal at this time of day. I headed for it, daring a glance behind as my pursuer rounded the corner. Several others had joined him. At the crest of the bridge, I peered over the side and spied a gondola filled with lemons floating lazily beneath me. Heaving myself onto the railing, I jumped and landed neatly in a pile of yellow fruit.

"Hey," the gondolier cried out, almost falling into the canal at the sight of an idiot boy squashing his wares. I did not stop to apologize but jumped from the offended man's boat to the lower balcony of the nearest palazzo, and from there I scaled along the wall to an alley which opened onto the canal.

By now my pursuers had reached the bridge and were trying to convince the boatman to take up the chase, hands waving, their voices rising in the air.

When my feet finally touched cobblestone, I ran. The commotion faded as I returned to my zigzagged escape.

Whether the ruffians ever convinced him to ferry them across, I have no idea. I continued my snaking run until my lungs ached and the surrounding streets no longer rang with any sounds of pursuit.

The great exertion and excitement at an end, I bent over, gasping. As my chest gradually ceased screaming, my stomach growled. The escape left me famished. My fingers fumbled in my pocket, empty.

The soldo was gone!

"So much for a blessing," I murmured angrily. No doubt the coin had fallen into the waters of the canal as I jumped from the bridge.

Venice had exacted her price for protecting me.

In the distance, the bells rang, signaling the end of the workday. I would catch a scolding, but I headed back to the Pietá to suffer my punishment and feed my empty stomach. It was best to avoid Nurse Francesca, so instead of heading in the front door, I scaled the outer balconies and tumbled headfirst through the window of my dormitory room. There was a chance I could convince my guardian I had been here all along.

THE GONDOLIER

The gondola rocked as a boy landed atop the fragrant pile of lemons weighing down the front of the boat. Jolted from his pleasant reverie, the gondolier sat up, indignation creasing his sallow face. People often threw things from the bridges, but a boy? It was too much! An angry cry escaped his lips as he made a swipe at the lad. But he swung too late and his hand caught only air. He shouted a stream of curses as the intruder catapulted himself out of the boat and onto a low balcony on the other side of the canal. Shaking his fist, the gondolier examined his precious cargo for damage.

A spark of light on the floor of the gondola caught the rower's eye. A coin. The youngster must have dropped it, for the gondolier had never had a whole soldo in his possession—his wife made sure of it. He opened his mouth to call out to the child but, for the first time, thinking before he spoke, he closed his lips. Picking the windfall up, he tossed the coin jauntily in the air. An extra glass or two of wine on his way home and his wife couldn't complain. She'd never know, and he would still be ahead with profits for the day. His mouth unfurled in a gap-toothed grin, and he slid the windfall into his pocket.

Ignoring the crowd gathered on the bridge watching the urchin's escape, he pushed his pole into the water and moved his craft away from the commotion, and towards a cup of comfort.

The day was wet, and inside the osteria simmered with humanity and smelled of sweat, burnt stew, and stale ale. The gondolier's dry mouth needed a drink. A glass of claret? He patted his pocket and sidled up to the bar. As usual he had eaten little and the effects of the wine would work quickly to warm him.

"Your finest claret," he told the barkeeper, sliding the soldo over the counter.

The barkeep picked up the coin, ran a finger over one flat side and bit it. The money seemed real. He tucked the payment into his pocket, grinning, and stroked his expansive waistcoat appreciatively. Then, reaching under the bar, he grasped a bottle of his cheapest wine.

"The best in the house!" he said, holding up the bottle and filling a generous cup. The gondolier grabbed the wine and drank with greedy appreciation.

One drink led to another, then another. More than a soldo's worth, in fact. The gondolier's wife would not be pleased. Closing time came sooner than expected, and he stumbled out the door and towards the canal where his gondola waited. The rain had left the cobbled streets slippery. As he fought to untie the saturated knot holding his boat secure, his feet slid on the slick ground. Tumbling forward, he hit his head against the slimy canal wall. Then, in slow motion, his body relaxed and sank into the water, barely making a ripple in the surface.

CHAPTER
3

It had been a week since Nurse Francesca had made her proclamation on my fate and I could not afford to lie low any longer if I was to put my own plans into action. I waited for my target by the corner of *Mercuria Orologio* and *Calle Fiubera*, a busy merchant area. The person I sought would pass by sometime. All I needed to do was wait.

My mind had been in turmoil since doubt was thrown on my prospects by my unfortunate run-in with Foscari. I could run away; sneaking away would be easy. But the possibility of constantly dodging the long arm of the caring nurses at Della Pietá was one I did not relish, and throwing angry nobles into the mix did not help matters. I would not go to Padua and pick olives, but to continue the life of relative freedom I enjoyed, I needed to find an appropriate substitute for Nurse Francesca's plan—appropriate in her eyes, that is—and a way to stay off the streets.

This was the circumstance which brought me now to this place, scanning the people for the face of an artist. His slight frame jostled through the crowded street. I chose my time carefully. He was just returning from the shops with fresh supplies for the studio. I tucked my hands into my pockets and, whistling, I approached him.

"Good day to you, Ser Bellini," I said.

Gentile Bellini was a member of the famous Bellini family. I had made it my business to acquaint myself with anyone who might be of influence in Venice. Artists, though usually poor, often had contact with the wealthiest families in the city. The Bellinis were no exception, and yet they did not consider themselves too important to speak to the likes of me.

True to his name, Gentile was more reserved than the overbearing Giovanni, his brother, or Jacopo, the exuberant patriarch. I had the best chance of persuading him of my usefulness to the family. At least his reserve would allow me to say my full piece without interruption.

"Nico," he responded, nodding, but continuing to move through the crowd.

"Let me help you," I said, offering to relieve him of his burden.

"Most kind of you." He handed over some unwieldy tubes, perhaps rolled canvases.

We walked along in silence for a few moments. Passersby jostled my packages, and I tightened my grip. Now was not the time to drop the artist canvases in the muck.

When our progress brought us to a less crowded part of the journey, I sighed. "It's too bad."

"What is too bad?" He adjusted some of his baggage, not looking at me, but too polite to ignore me completely.

"The waste of your valuable time running errands. I am most sure this is time you would much rather spend painting." I lifted my shoulders at the injustice of the situation.

"Well, it is necessary." His pace quickened, perhaps reminded by my words of more important tasks or because the street ahead of us emptied.

"It would be good for you to have some help in this area," I added as I jogged to keep up with his long stride.

"I would trust no one else picking out my dyes and canvases."

Venice was the best place in the entire world to find dyes and colorings for artists. Our strategic position along world trade routes ensured the best quality products were always available. Venetian painters were renowned for the vibrant colors of their paintings.

"You could train someone," I suggested as if the idea had just occurred to me. I shifted the packages I held. We had reached the front door of the Studio Bellini.

"I suppose I could," he responded. His face did not betray any emotion, but his gaze rested on me. "You are here to offer your services?"

He saw through my subterfuge, but I had known he would. To show respect, I did not come right out and ask.

"I am most eager to learn. I think you would find me an efficient and compliant pupil."

"Is this how your last masters found you?" The question was a fair one, and lying would have been easy.

Squirming slightly, I had the grace to blush. "I am sure I would be much more compatible with your family than with my previous positions."

He laughed. "I think you may use your wit in our favor. Perhaps securing us better bargains on our supplies with your subtle flattery. Very well, I will speak with my father. If he is agreeable, I will inquire at the Pietá about acquiring your services."

"I am not happy about this," Nurse Francesca said when she called me to her a few days later. "I am sure sending you out of Venice is a much safer plan. However, I dislike disappointing such a well-respected family. But"—she paused and glared at me with such ferocity my face stung— "if you embarrass me, you will wish an olive farm in Padua had been your fate."

CHAPTER
4

I settled into the routine of the Bellinis' workshop. With Nurse Francesca's threats still ringing in my ears, I tried my best to excel at my duties. Some were dull: washing brushes and sweeping up the workshop, but delivery boy persisted my favorite, by far.

Being out of the workshop and running free in the streets was pure joy to me. My intimate knowledge of the city allowed me to complete my duties hastily, leaving plenty of time to roam the marketplaces, pick a few pockets, and return when most of the tedious jobs were done.

Gentile had yet to fulfill his promise of instructing me in the art of procuring dyes and canvas. Ser Jacopo kept threatening to teach me to paint, but Ser Giovanni claimed I had all the talent of a canal rat.

Not long after I had become a permanent installment at the workshop, the city of Venice prepared to welcome the new doge.

"Ser Bellini," I called, swinging the door open and entering.

The studio of the Bellini family bustled with life. The pungent scent of paint and wet canvas filled my nostrils. On one side, two novices stood poised in front of easels, nursing looks of intense concentration. The senior Bellini, Jacopo, hovered behind them, hand to his chin. To study with the Bellinis remained the greatest privilege an artist in Venice could hope for.

In the center of the room a young woman lay, stretched out on a couch, draped with multi-colored silk coverings which puddled on the floor. A lilac sheet snaked over her form, covering much of her creamy white skin. I averted my eyes and wiped a small bead of sweat from my upper lip.

The master looked up from the work of his students as the door shut with a hollow clang. "Nico." He nodded. "We are glad to see you!"

Before I could answer, Signora Bellini, a woman of no small proportions, bustled in.

"Dinner is ready, Jacopo, time to put the paints away." She spied me and greeted me, hands raised. "Nico, where have you been?" Casting a glance at the occupied couch, she grabbed my shoulders and turned me towards the kitchen, throwing her husband a wicked look. "Into the kitchen with you. Really, Jacopo, can't you learn to lock the door when you are painting..." Her eyes darted to the young woman now sitting up and wrapping the sheet around herself.

"No, no, don't move," Jacopo protested, but the rest of his words faded as the kindly lady placed firm hands on my shoulders and propelled me into the kitchen. The door closed behind me.

The scent of garlic and herbs woke my hollow stomach, and an extended rumble emanated from my mid-section.

"When was the last time you ate?" The good lady frowned, and I shrugged.

The table creaked under the weight of her plentiful cooking. Pasta, cheese, bread, and olives appeared as if by magic. The Master, Gentile, Giovanni, the young apprentices, and even the young lady—now clad in a loose-fitting robe—joined us at the table. We ate until our stomachs could hold no more.

"I talked to Lord Foscari about the portrait of Doge Mocenigo," Giovanni said, wiping oily fingers on his shirt and burping to show his satisfaction.

The taste of the lady's excellent food turned to sawdust in my mouth at the sound of Foscari's name. I choked on the salty eel I had just bitten into. Signora Bellini jumped up in alarm. She slapped me on the back and held my arms above my head.

"Come, boy," Giovanni said when I regained my breath. "You have been silent this meal, which has been a relief for some of us. Do you now seek to gain attention by choking to death, you simpleton?"

Giovanni always talked like this. I took no offense as, compared to him, I *was* simple. Now, however, with olive picking looming large in my mind, I had to impress these good people. I was failing thus far.

"The new doge, how wonderful!" Signora Bellini exclaimed. She was anxious to return to a topic of conversation more appealing to her. "It's such an honor. The Bellini family is so admired by the Great Council."

"The honor will be all theirs, to hang another Bellini painting in the Ducal Palace," Jacopo grunted, but his eyes twinkled.

"As long as it's just a Bellini *painting* they are hanging," Gentile quipped in his soft voice.

Giovanni snorted in amusement. Of the two brothers, Giovanni had the better reputation as a painter. But Gentile received the call to the palace to immortalize the newest doges in paint; he was the official portrait painter to the Council. Thus, it was a great honor for me to be schooled by this illustrious, although not wealthy, family. I did not wish to be a painter, but my association with them could increase my chances at a successful career. I determined to make the most of my opportunities.

"THE PARADE for the installation is tomorrow. I think Nico should attend. After all, he had a hand in choosing our new leader," Jacopo announced while we enjoyed our noon meal.

"Good, we can blame him when circumstances go awry." Giovanni laughed uproariously at his own joke. "Will you dress as an angel and march with the other children?"

I scowled but turned my face to the floor, so he would not see. I wanted to keep my post here, but sometimes Ser Giovanni's sense of humor made it difficult, accustomed as I was to voicing my own thoughts.

It would please Father Vincenzo to know I had improved in my ability to hold my tongue, however painful the process. Now, if only my fingers were not so often in other people's pockets, he would have reason to be proud of me.

"Nico and I will view the spectacle together," Ser Gentile said. "I want a chance to watch Doge Mocenigo unposed. It will be helpful to have Nico there to carry my sketching materials."

My excitement waned slightly in Ser Gentile's presence. My pockets had been empty of late, my salary of apprenticeship being limited to food, tutelage, and a small sum given directly to the charitable sisters at the Pietá. And I still smarted under the loss of my soldo.

Of the three Bellini painters, Gentile was my favorite. Giovanni's raw wit and love of making a joke at another's expense made him harder to take. Gentile's demeanor was quiet, thoughtful, and gentle. These three characteristics, foreign to me, drew me to him. But if I was to replace my lost fortunes, I could not be under his sharp eye. Still, a day in the

Piazza San Marco, with all of Venice showing its finery, thrilled my soul. The crowd would make it easy for me to become *accidentally* separated from the painter.

I hurried through my evening tasks, hoping my poor performance would go unnoticed in the dim light. Brushes, stones for grinding pigments, mastic, and bits of foil and paper lay about the room. A light tap at the door interrupted my labors. Relieved at the chance to desert my duties, I hurried to answer it. The late hour of the visit did not surprise me. Guests popped in unannounced frequently, for the Bellini family was much beloved in Venice.

I unlatched the door and opened it, fully expecting some young noble and his lady stopping by for a drink and a bit of conversation. Instead, it was the scowling face of Lord Foscari. I stepped back and banged into Gentile, who had come up quietly behind me, no doubt summoned by the knock.

The noble ignored me—as any well-born would—and directed his oily smile to Gentile. My neck prickled as his gaze swept over the workshop. Stepping back into the shadows, I hoped to remain unnoticed. This man was dangerous. Inwardly, I berated myself for not having played dumb when our eyes met over the dropped wax ball. I could have easily put on the face of a simpleton. I had done it many times before. But something in me loathed a cheater. And a cheat he surely was.

"Lord Foscari," Gentile greeted him formally. Gentile never gushed in the manner of Giovanni. "Please enter. The evening is cool."

Foscari nodded and entered the big front room. He removed his cloak and gloves, depositing them in my arms without so much as a flick of an eye in my direction.

"I have come to speak of the new doge's portrait. You have agreed to paint it?"

"Please sit," Gentile said, motioning to a chair. "Nico, get our guest a drink. Wine?"

"Claret." Foscari nodded, taking a seat.

I hurried into the kitchen, pleased to be out of Foscari's noxious presence. When Signora Bellini heard of our visitor, she clucked her usual cluck, showing either pleasure or pain, as applied to the situation. I had convinced her to return to the workshop with the refreshments herself when she spied her reflection in the shiny surface of the kettle she polished.

"Oh, Nico, I look an absolute mess," she exclaimed, attempting to tame her wild hair. "I am not going out there looking like this. You take the tray."

Reluctantly, I took the small tray from her hands, my pleadings no match for her pride. I backed through the door and turned to where the two men sat discussing Gentile's design for the new portrait. I placed the tray, with two goblets and a small dish of nuts, on the table where both men could reach it. As neither took any notice of me I moved away, intending to return to the kitchen.

"You may continue your tasks, Nico. You will not disturb us. I will need the studio well organized for tomorrow's pupils."

"Yes, Ser Bellini," I mumbled, keeping my back to them. I returned to my chores, trying to be as quiet as I could. But all the same, I listened closely to what they said.

"It is quite an honor for you, Gentile, to paint our Most Serene Prince."

"I have painted doges before," Gentile said, his voice neutral.

"Yes. However, this doge is of an outstanding nature. It is glorious news, is it not? I too have been honored to be selected a member of the Council of Ten. Perhaps God has put me in this position for a greater purpose."

"You are to be congratulated," Gentile remarked, a hint of impatience in his voice.

Anger rose in my veins like floodwaters in winter. The Council of Ten was the inmost circle and confidant of the doge. Foscari had cheated his way into this place, and for him to pretend God had ordained it made bile rise in my throat. Both he and I knew well it was through his own vile trickery he had secured the honor. I tightened my hand around the rough handle of the paintbrush I was cleaning, imagining it was the odious man's neck.

He continued as if Gentile had not spoken. "I wish to be sure this portrait is a tribute to God and man. I want only the finest of materials, of course."

"Naturally. I have received some excellent ingredients for paints lately. I am sure they will suit. Nico," Gentile called. "Bring me a piece of the lapis lazuli Giovanni bought last week. I want to show Lord Foscari."

Clenching my jaw at the need to perform even this minor task for Foscari, I turned to look at the shelves. It was easy to locate the small piece of rock.

"This will make a lovely rich purple," Gentile said.

I crossed the room and avoided looking at the other man as I held the stone out to Gentile.

"No, no," he said, waving me away. "Give it to Lord Foscari so he can see the quality for himself."

Hand outstretched, I rotated towards Foscari.

His face was smug. The smile, slick and greasy, oozed with confidence and superiority. But I knew what he was. And I could not allow him to think his misdeeds would never surface again. I held out the rock, and his hand opened to receive it. Leaning forward, I dropped the stone just beyond his open palm. It hit the floor with a small thud and rolled slightly before it came to rest.

"Fool," Foscari snapped. Slowly, agonizingly, he raised his eyes from the floor where Gentile crawled, now muttering and scrambling to pick up the wayward stone, and rested his gaze upon me. "Can't you watch—" The words froze on his lips.

I did not lower my eyes or turn my head. He held me fully in his possession now, seeing me for the first time. He knew me. Yes, he knew me.

Gentile rose from the floor and spoke, though I know not what he said, so intense was Foscari and my bondage with each other.

Foscari was the first to break the connection. "Ah, our orphan is your apprentice!" His voice was light, but it ripped through my body like cold steel. I had wakened the sleeping tiger.

"Yes," Gentile responded. Did his eyes dart from Foscari to me, or did I imagine it? "Nico told us of the honor given him during the election of our most Serene Prince."

"Indeed? And what did he tell you of his experience?" Foscari held the lapis lazuli in his hand now. He gazed at it with intent as he turned it in his palm.

"It was an honor he would remember all his life."

It was perhaps the worst thing said. As the realization of my folly dawned on me, I groaned inwardly.

"But I think sleep is making him clumsy. Off to bed with you, right now." Ser Gentile shooed me away.

"You must bring him with you when you begin the portraiture. A boy as observant as he could learn much from such a task." He handed the rock back to Gentile, rubbing his hands together to remove any specks of color remaining. Then, carefully, he drew on his gloves. I glanced back as I left the room and saw his gaze was still upon me.

THE BARKEEP

The barkeep wiped the counter. A rainy night always meant a busy night. The till was full, a comfortable feeling.

"You! Wipe it up," he barked at the weary server. She didn't answer but picked up a bucket of brown water and swabbed up the mess with a torn rag, filthier than the floor itself. He watched her work until she finished.

The barkeep wiped his hands on his waistcoat and felt the bulge in his pocket. Reaching a finger in, he pulled out a soldo. It glinted faintly in the candlelight. He gave it a rub with his thumb, pausing on the flattened side for a moment.

"The take was good today?" The woman's voice grated in his ears. Her eyes pierced the soldo he held up.

"No." He turned from her and slid the coin back in his pocket. "Many didn't pay, most just stayed to nurse their drinks."

It wasn't true, and as she turned from him, he saw her mouthing a curse under her breath. There would be no extra coin in her wages.

He was the last to leave, locking the door and hiding the heavy jingling sack of coins under his coat as he stepped into the cold drizzle. He was always careful, even on a night like this. A little rain would not deter thieves.

Darkness clogged the alley, and a faint scuffle reached his ear a moment too late.

With a thump on his head, he fell like a sack to the ground. The scuffling was louder for a moment, and then the jingling *sound echoed in the corridor as the thieves scurried off with his bag of coins.*

CHAPTER 5

The piazza, like an artist's palette, was awash with colors. By nature, Venetians are sober people, but festival times in the city surpass the greatest fêtes in all Christendom. The standard royal red and gold of the Lion of St. Mark replaced black. The narrow streets rang with the sound of bells as every church in every quarter entered the jollity. The smell of fish cooking over open coals, smothered with garlic, onions, and spices, rode the wind like elegant perfume. And the salty sea air seasoned everything to perfection.

The election of a new doge was one of the greatest festivities in the city's life. A grand parade topped the gaiety, circling the Piazza San Marco like a dragon on the wing. All of Venice turned out, decked in their finest, to bless our new ruler.

When we reached the piazza, the Grand Procession had not yet begun, so we searched for a good vantage point from which to watch the proceedings.

"Here, boy." Gentile motioned me to the center of the square. "They will walk the outer edge. Set up my easel here; we will see everything." As he spoke, the nasal sound of the trumpets rent the air. The priests threw the doors of Basilica

San Marco open, and the procession poured from its innards, like a giant snake escaping its skin.

First came the priests, in their white robes, burning sweet smelling incense which wafted a floral haze over the square. Next, a merry band of musicians playing a lilting tune sauntered by, flute and trumpet mingling together in happy harmony. Every foot tapped a jig as the feather capped musicians played, faces red and fingers dancing up and down the chords. Nobles, in velvet and brocade, stood shoulder to shoulder with humble peasants in brown linen trousers.

A troupe of children dressed as white, robed angels followed the musicians. Their wings dropped feathers like delicate snow as they went. Amongst this angelic choir, I recognized Stefano.

"Stefano!"

He swiveled his head towards me, then he ducked out of the group and came to join us.

"You look the picture of angelic beauty." I grinned, taking in his white robe and lopsided halo.

He punched me none too gently in the stomach. "Mind your manners, or it's ten more years in purgatory for you," Stefano said, his mouth turned down in a scowl. "Nurse Francesca made us."

"Looks like I escaped just in time."

"Yes." Stefano nodded grimly. "Another week and I would have been spared this humiliation at least."

"Oh?" I queried.

"Yes, my uncle comes to fetch me."

"Really?"

"We had word last week. Apparently, he did not know I had survived the illness which took my parents. As soon as he found out, he sent word he would come."

"Wonderful news," I exclaimed, slapping his winged back. "Where does your uncle live?"

"Sicily."

"Sicily! So you will leave Venice?"

"Yes, soon. I don't know when."

I pumped his arm and congratulated him again, but I felt sorry for him. To leave Venice—it was a tragedy. I would sooner be an orphan in Venice than the son of a king elsewhere.

Nurse Francesca spotted her wayward charge and hurried over. "Stefano, what an example to set for the young ones," she scolded, then she spotted me. "Nico! So good to see you! And Ser Bellini, how fares our little apprentice?"

"He does well," Gentile replied with a smile. "We are most pleased with his progress; I will make a painter out of him yet."

Nurse Francesca smiled, but only one side of her mouth curled up, the look she often gave me when listening to my feeble attempts to explain away my behavior. For once, we agreed. Taking her leave, she hurried Stefano back to join the heavenly host.

A cheer went up from the crowd.

The doge had emerged from the church. Dressed in an ermine cloak and wearing his golden berretta, he descended the steps of the basilica and joined the procession. The crowd yelled enthusiastically, mostly good wishes with a few bawdy comments thrown in by those who had taken more than communion wine. The sound of the *Te Deum laudamus* draped the crowd in sacred music, making holy even what was not.

A lump grew in my throat. Truly, in the entire world there existed no better place than the *Stato de Mare,* and here I stood at the center of the center of the world. The golden Lion of St. Mark looked down upon the scene from the basilica roof where it stood, wings wide in glorious majesty. I could almost hear a roar as if the statue were alive.

A familiarly odious voice interrupted my thoughts as a hand clamped down upon my shoulder.

"Gentile," Foscari said, jovially. "A joyous day! And here is Nico, the boy who started it all."

His grip on my shoulder tightened, his fingertips digging painfully into my skin. I tried to worm free, but he held firm.

"You will begin the portraiture soon?" His eyes fixed on Ser Gentile while his hand stayed on my shoulder.

"This week." Gentile nodded.

"And no doubt you will bring Nico to help." This was the second time the spider had invited the fly to dine. My enemy drew the web tighter.

They exchanged a few more pleasantries and Foscari departed, giving my shoulder one more painful squeeze.

"It seems you have made quite an impression on Lord Foscari," Gentile said as we walked back to the workshop. "Strange he should be so eager for you to accompany me."

What could I say? I would not tell him what Foscari had done. And even if I did, it would make little difference.

"You are wise to keep your own council. But remember, Nico, you are not alone anymore."

"But I haven't ever been alone. The Lord has always been with me."

Gentile's face curled in a slow and thoughtful smile. "My error, you are correct, lad."

THE SERVING WOMAN

From a dark corner of the alley, the serving woman emerged. The sound of scuffling had brought her back to the bar. She walked over to the barkeep, who lay on his side on the wet cobblestones. His chest moved; life remained in him. The coin glinted as it rolled from his pocket.

She picked it up. A soldo.

"Only what you owe me, old man." She gave a haughty sniff and dropped the coin into her bag.

She pushed him gingerly with one toe. He let out a low moan. Someone would find him in the morning. It wouldn't hurt the old skin flint to spend a night cold and wet. The Holy Saints knew she had been cold and wet often enough. Pulling her scarf over her head, she hurried off into the darkness.

At home, she threw herself onto the unmade bed in the small filthy room and lay unconscious until the morning sun filtered through the cracks in the shutters, warming the bed on which she lay. She rolled over and groaned, eyeing the space next to her.

"Is there any breakfast?" A small, thin voice floated into her ear.

She swatted it away. "Not unless you got a job," she snapped at the girl standing by the bed.

"I made you tea, Mother," the girl answered, holding up a chipped pottery cup, steam rising from the lip.

"I told you not to use the fire unless I was awake. You could burn us in our beds."

The girl cowered at the harsh words, but still held up the cup.

The woman snatched it and slurped at the hot liquid. It tasted like water.

"Did you put any tea in this?" She spat the offending liquid on the floor.

The girl shook her head. "There was none."

"I am going to take you to the Pietá today," the woman said, heaving herself reluctantly from the bed.

"Oh, Mother, please no." The girl ran forward and knelt on one knee, hands grasping the woman's skirt.

"I told you not to call me Mother." The woman shook off the hands roughly. "I'm not your mother."

The girl whimpered but said no more. The one who was not her mother opened a wooden box on the bedside table. She took out a folded piece of paper. There were words written on it, but the woman could not read them. The priest wrote them for her. A note to the hospital, telling them she could no longer care for the child. Why had she ever agreed to take it in the first place? The mother had been so pathetic, so in love with the brat, it touched the woman, for a moment. Maybe the child would bring some love into her life. Of course, it hadn't. Another mouth to feed; an annoyance, always there, always wanting, never giving the woman what she needed.

The priest said they would not take the child without some kind of payment. The woman took the soldo out of her bag. Well, it would be a wrench to give it up, but doing so meant everything she earned from now on would be for herself. No more sharing, no other mouth to feed. Life would be better, easier. She wrapped the coin in the paper and put it into her pocket.

"Come on, we are going out," she told the girl.

"To the hospital?" The child's voice quavered. Her obvious fear annoyed the woman.

"Quickly."

The girl picked up a torn shawl to wrap around her thin shoulders.

"Leave the shawl alone, it's mine." The woman grabbed the tattered garment from the girl and threw it around her own shoulders. The two hurried out into the bright morning sunlight.

CHAPTER
6

My encounter with Foscari in the Piazza San Marco left me unsettled. I lay awake listening to the lapping of the canal outside my window. My room was a small storage closet off the kitchen. Not a room, really, only a space where I could go to be out of sight. A luxury not permitted in the orphan hospital, and one which I cherished beyond my own expectations. Even the thin mat on the floor, which was my bed, far inferior to the wooden cot I was used to, did not dampen my enthusiasm for this small space. There was a window which looked out over Signora Bellini's small herb garden towards the *Rio de la Fava*. When sleep escaped me, I would hoist myself out of the window and sit by the edge of the canal, dipping my toes in the water. The salty blackness swirling around my feet soothed me.

Tonight, I found no comfort in my ritual. The grasp of Mother Venice was tight on me, and in the dim moonlight it pulled me towards something, though I knew not what. Foscari was a cheat, but he was only one man on the Council of Ten. Only one of the four hundred other men of influence on the Great Council. I wondered why he had done it. There was a risk, after all. The price of public shame was a high one to pay.

This question plagued me and caused me sleeplessness. I

had, as far as I could see, no way to determine his motives or his plans, if he had any. And there was no need for me to. Yet the feeling nagged at me, unrelentingly. As if the reluctant angels were again at my ear whispering, entreating me to intervene, and Mother Venice egged them on. It was almost intolerable.

I toyed with the idea of stalking him. Lying outside his window and listening to his mutterings as he slept. The idea was ludicrous. Besides, he would now be on the lookout for me. I knew he would try again to warn me away. And the warning would not be with a gentle word. I expected violence of some nature. It irked how someone of his obvious advantage should gain an even greater privilege. I admired ambition, and yet I did not find this man admirable.

The obsidian water of the canal was menacing. A shiver ran up my spine. At the unexpected sound of footsteps, the back of my neck prickled. I jumped up, straining my eyes to peer into the gloom. A shadow slipped by the garden gate. In a single bound, I catapulted myself through the open window and tumbled heavily upon my mat. Heart pumping and head sore from connecting with the floor, I listened. There was no sound of an intruder, no splash of an oar or tap of a shoe echoing in the deserted streets.

I slammed the shutter tight on the window and threw the clasp.

As the hammering in my chest slowed, anger replaced fear. A life spent diving from shadows did not appeal.

Head back and jaw clenched, I opened the shutters once more and peered out into the night, daring the ghouls to show themselves. The courtyard was as quiet as Sunday prayers, and the shadow of fear dispelled.

I allowed myself a moment to consider. It was clear there was but one thing to do: face the *bocche dei leone*, The Lion's Mouth.

There were several of these grotesque slots throughout the city where a citizen could accuse his neighbor of any number of deeds, from petty theft to murder. A simple note slipped into the mouth could cast suspicion on guilty and innocent alike. The letter must be signed by the accuser and by two witnesses, but my plan was to ignore this. I need only to cast suspicion on Foscari, make those around him cautious. That would be enough.

It is a simple task to obtain a scrap of parchment in the workshop of an artist. I had no trouble in finding a paper and ink upon which to write my accusation of Lord Foscari. Any orphan under the charge of Nurse Francesca had at least the most rudimentary knowledge of writing skills, and I had been an eager student; a successful merchant must read, write, and calculate well. My note was brief, only explaining what I knew and not who I was or why I knew it. Anyone who had been at the palazzo that day could have written the letter.

The next morning, armed with the letter in my pocket, I headed out into the *campo* on several errands for Gentile. As I rounded the corner into *Mercuria Orologio* there was a man leaning against the wall outside the goldsmiths. He moved, unconcerned, into step behind me.

In Piazza San Marco, he continued to dog my steps. My muscles tensed, alert now. I zigzagged across the open square. He was never far away. Ducking into the basilica, I hid behind a large pillar. In the dim light, I kept my eyes fixed on the door. A shadow blocked the sunlight as the man entered, looking around.

The tension in my muscles crawled up the back of my neck and settled in my temple. I was being followed. The terrors of the night before took hold of me once more. Breathless, I waited for him to leave. The moments seemed frozen. Nothing moved. After an eternity, he turned and exited the way he had come in.

My palms were wet with sweat and my hands shook as I dug them deep into my pockets.

THROUGHOUT THE REST of the day and into the next, mysterious looking figures tailed me. In my pocket, the parchment grew worn and crumpled. I seemed never to be alone. If I approached one of the familiar bocche, a figure was sure to be near, watching. It became obvious the only way to achieve my goal without interference would be under the cover of darkness. The sooner I completed my task, the sooner Foscari would be under suspicion, the sooner I could return to my own affairs.

I waited for the first moonless night.

Gentile noticed my agitation. "Nico, what is wrong with you? I have told you three times already the address for this delivery."

I shrugged and tried to look ill. "I am not feeling well, master."

"Not feeling well on this beautiful spring day?" Gentile tilted his head and furrowed his brow. My stomach clenched, guilty at the lie. "What a shame. Perhaps you should rest?"

I shook my head. I would not cower in my room. Setting my shoulders back, I answered him. "No, no, I am sure a little exercise and air will do me well."

Gentile nodded but did not cease to gaze upon my face. I squirmed under his scrutiny; my powers of deception were slipping.

The moon was only a small silver arc, throwing no light into the darkened corridors of the city. I wore no shoes to be silent on my journey through the cobblestone streets. Although there were several bocche dei leone throughout the city, I chose one several miles' distance from the workshop. I wanted to put space between the accusation and myself.

The night was cool, and so quiet, except for the scratching sound of rats carrying out their evening scrounging. Even my own breathing echoed in my ears.

In the silence, a clattering arose behind me. My body turned to stone. A sharp voice swore and then all was quiet again. The night remained still. It was long before I moved again. I counted each turn I took on the twisted route. I did not want followers.

It took me two terror-filled hours to reach my destination. In the darkness, I could just make out the place where the mouth of the lion gaped. I slid my hand into my pocket and touched the crumpled paper, still where it had lived this past week. Pulling it out, I reached into the black hole. As I scraped my knuckles against the stone teeth, a loud scuffling caused me to jump. I opened my fingers and release my missive, and in one motion, turned and ran. I took no pains to hide my course or be silent as I had on my outward journey; my only goal was to return to the workshop unmolested. If I had a pursuer, there would be no secret where I was going. I had to get there first.

I could not tell if I was being chased, because my ears were full of the sound of my blood pounding through my veins. My breath came in piercing gasps as rough as sand in my lungs, and my tense muscles screamed in agony. I strained for the familiar sight of *Campo San Lio* and the Bellinis' front door.

When it came into view, my lagging strength returned. Throwing myself forward, I rounded the side of the small house and catapulted into the window from which I had escaped. Footsteps echoed in the street, but it might only have been the sound of my own bones clattering together.

The deed accomplished, I was through with Foscari.

THE GIRL

The bony fingers of the older woman dug into the girl's arm as she pulled the child through the rough streets.

"Here." The woman thrust something into the girl's hand.

A hard lump wrapped in paper lay in her palm.

"You are to give the coin to the nurse after I leave. It's for your upkeep."

The girl folded her hand over the lump.

A stooped figure in a black robe, the uniform of all Venetians, approached. "Hello, dearie, where are you off to in such a hurry?"

"None of your business, old fool," the woman said as she continued to move forward.

"Is she your child?" the man asked, pointing one claw in the girl's direction.

An unpleasant wave of heat swept over her body as the bony finger waggled her way. She tried to step back, sensing danger. The blood pumping through her thin body moved faster, a flush of fear washed over her. Whatever happened she knew she must keep as far away from this menace as possible.

"Not for long." The woman slowed her pace so the crooked figure could keep step with them, sensing opportunity.

"Pity, times are tough," he said, nodding his head. Strands of wispy grey hair bobbed underneath his hood. To the girl those wisps seemed like tiny snakes, hissing and undulating at her. "I never was a grandfather myself, more's the shame. An old man longs for the comfort of youth in these dark days."

The woman stopped. "What would you offer me for her?" She squinted at him.

He wavered. "I have little..." He held his shriveled hands wide to emphasize the truth of his words.

"I might want her back, eventually," she said. Her eyes darted to the girl's hand. "She's worth something to me."

The old fellow chuckled and opened his toothless mouth wide. "I can see there is a lot of love between you and the child, although she looks nothing like you."

The woman snorted. "Ugly brat, I know, but I have a mother's heart."

"Very well. Let your mother's heart be at rest. I will keep her well until your maternal instincts reassert themselves." They both laughed rudely, and the woman shoved the girl towards the old demon.

"Go on, he's your father now. Well, grandfather, maybe."

The girl stood stock still, eyes wide, staring at the wizened figure. Rot and decay issued from his drooping smile. The full horror of the moment came upon her, and her mouth opened.

She let out a scream.

The sound was indistinct, at first, as tiny as the squeal of a mouse. But the force of it grew louder and shriller until it engulfed the alley. The shriek ricocheted off the stone walls surrounding them, climbing higher and higher towards the blue, blue sky.

The old man covered his ears. "Ye gods!" He cringed as the noise split his head like a sword slicing a watermelon.

"Stop it, stop it," the woman growled, reaching out to smack the girl.

But her hand struck only air, for the child was no longer there, and the high piercing sound cut off as the power of the shriek was refocused into escape. Her bare feet made no noise on the stones as she ran.

In an instant, she vanished.

"My soldo," the wretched crone cried as she realized what she had lost.

CHAPTER
7

I dragged the heavy wagon over the bumpy street. It rattled like a broken shutter in the wind. I ground my teeth in annoyance at Gentile's complete ignorance of my struggle. He hurried before me as if the weight of countless brushes, paints, and canvasses did not encumber me.

It was pointless to protest, though. Silent and morose was the demeanor he adopted whenever he planned a work. The process of creation possessed his being and the physical world left him like dried leaves cast out in a breeze. Any words I might utter would be of no more importance to him than the braying of a donkey.

Sweat beaded on my brow, as the day was unusually hot for the season. The winter was waning, and a new season tickled my nose with the scent of warm earth. In the height of summertime, when the canals had been simmering in the sun, the odor of human waste and rotting fish would overpower even a nose-less leper. But it was barely spring, and the waterways were not yet cooked as in the heat of summer. The crisp air was scented by the briny sea. I inhaled, filling my lungs with this goodness, and tried to keep my mind clear for the task at hand.

We headed to the Palazzo Ducal to begin the royal portrait.

Doge Mocenigo did not come to the workshop for a sitting. The most important of the clientele remained in their own surroundings. Ser Gentile strode ahead, deep in thought. I could have called the curse of a thousand elephants upon his head and he would have taken no notice.

For the second time in my brief life, I entered the grand palazzo. The guards ushered us to a private chamber to wait for Doge Mocenigo.

Doge Giovanni Mocenigo had been in office for less than a month, but he had the air of a man accustomed to his position. As I set up the supplies, Ser Gentile and the doge discussed the arrangement for the portrait, composition, and lighting. I studied the elder statesman as I worked. Thrilling sensations coursed through my body as I beheld this most illustrious Venetian.

When the painting began, the doge sat erect. His *corno*, like an upside-down trumpet, made his head look larger and longer than was natural. His eyes, slightly sunken in the sockets, roamed the room under papery lids. It was usual for the doge to be of an advanced age. Mocenigo was at least seventy, but he had the bearing of a younger man. At the corners of his eyes, thin lines feathered out. His ornate cloak was closed at the neck with an acorn-shaped clasp, most probably in pure gold itself. Here was a man who knew much. I searched my brain for a way to make the most of my time in his presence. His movements, the words he used, the way he gazed with interest upon Gentile as the artist spoke exuded confidence. I attempted to hold my hands as he did and straightened my back to imitate his regal air.

These attempts so engrossed my attention I did not realize someone was calling my name. I came back to awareness to find both the painter and the Doge staring in my direction. My face reddened; I had not been paying attention to my tasks. This was not the way to impress.

"The child has departed this world for a moment. Where had you gone, lad?"

The doge was addressing me. Doge Mocenigo was addressing me, a poor orphan boy without even a name. The gravity of the situation left me speechless.

"You have a mute pupil, Ser Bellini?" he queried, looking to the painter.

"I am not mute," I answered. "My apologies; my mind was pondering the wonder of a person such as myself being in a place such as this." I waved my hand around vaguely at our surroundings.

"Indeed? And what sort of a person are you?"

"I am nobody, just an orphan, of no importance."

"You are important to yourself, are you not?"

"Yes, I am, your honor, but of no importance to Venice."

"Unfortunately, I must correct you again. Every Venetian is important to our city. It is through every citizen who values our way of life, Venice can find the succor to survive."

I marveled at this; he chose to speak to me. His correction and encouragement buoyed my confidence.

"You do intend to live your life as a true Venetian, do you not?" he continued.

"Yes, I do, your honor."

"And what do you see yourself as? A painter, perhaps?"

"Oh no, your honor, I have no talent. The Bellini family is infinitely kind to have apprenticed me, but they are truly only showing the most fulsome charity in doing so."

"Then what?"

"I would like to become a merchant, selling these fine pigments Ser Bellini has taught me about."

"Do you wish to travel the world, like Marco Polo?"

"Not at all," I answered. "What finer things could I see than this?"

He threw back his head and laughed, and Ser Bellini made a small noise of irritation in his throat. My master had little patience for anyone, Most Serene Princes included, while he painted. The doge must have heard the noise, for he turned his head to the artist.

"Ser Bellini, I may steal your apprentice. He seems a wise lad."

"Indeed," the painter answered. "But please, Most Serene Prince, keep still."

"Forgive me for making your job more difficult." The doge said no more but gave me a slight wink.

I did not wink back, but I must admit being tempted, though it might land me in the Leads—Venice's most infamous of prisons—for my impudence.

To paint a portrait takes many days, and Ser Bellini and I were in the palace often. Our routine was always the same; I would set up the master's tools, while the doge would ply me with questions about matters weighty and small. Sometimes his queries were ordinary and sometimes they were strange, but my answers amused him. When Ser Bellini raised his brush, the questioning was over, and the doge would settle into silence.

Once my tasks were complete, I would sit and ponder my prospects. I imagined one day the doge would knock at the door of the workshop and declare he must have me for his apprentice.

The last day at the palace was a hot one. The doge's mood was not as jovial as it had been in the past. He was large and prone to feeling the heat. Sweat rolled down his forehead and he fanned himself frequently despite the painter's reminders to remain still.

"Gads, man, is this infernal picture not done yet? I am roasting in this blessed cloak," he growled.

"You may remove the cloak," Ser Gentile responded, paying

no attention to his subject's obvious annoyance. The cloak was removed and, to my horror, he used it to wipe his wet brow.

"Here, boy, take this to my chambers." He held the heavy garment out to me. I took the cloak in my arms. "Mind you don't lose the clasp," he called after me as I left the room.

I had used the days here wisely and contrived to get to know the palazzo well. The doge often sent me on errands to fetch water or carry a message. As I hurried along the corridor towards his private chamber, I hoped someone would be there to receive the garment. I knocked firmly on the door and waited for it to open. When it did not, I tried the handle; it was unlocked.

Leaving the door open, I entered the room and carefully hung the cloak over the back of a chair, making sure the acorn clasp was closed tightly so it might not fall off. I turned to leave and almost collided with a body entering the room.

"Fah, what the devil," an angry voice cried. I found my bearings and peered up at the offended speaker. My stomach plummeted.

"What are you doing here?" Foscari barked.

"I am returning the highness' cloak, as he asked me. No one was here to receive it, so I entered and put it there." I spoke in a low but steady voice.

"But why are *you* here, at the palace?" The words shot out of his mouth like a whip.

"My master is painting the doge." I kept my head down, my eyes on his boots as a truly respectful servant would. The top of my head heated under his gaze. He was silent for several moments.

"Very well. You have done your job; get back to where you belong. And watch out for your betters." He cuffed me roughly on the side of the head and waited for me to depart.

I needed no urging; turning, I made my way back to where

my master waited. I had been feeling somewhat melancholy. The master was almost done, and we would be leaving the palace soon. But this encounter had expunged my reluctance to leave. Still, Foscari had said nothing out of the usual for a man of his stature to a servant of mine. Perhaps he had forgotten the incident, forgotten me. I could only hope. His presence here was evidence my letter into the bocche dei leone had not done its work. Still, perhaps this was for the best.

CHAPTER
8

There is little more fateful than a knock on a door.

I was busy at my daily tasks when the tap came. I opened the door to a liveried page waiting outside.

"A message for Ser Gentile Bellini, from Doge Mocenigo," the young lad said. His attire was smart, and he gave me a look which spoke of his assurance of superiority. My knuckles ached to wipe the smirk off his face, but I merely nodded and retired to fetch the master.

"Your presence is needed at the palace," the boy announced when Ser Gentile arrived.

"What for?" He was always cranky in the morning.

"I don't know, Ser, but he says to bring him with you." He pointed at me.

Joy rose in my chest and a smug smile must have played on my lips, for the lad scowled.

"Oh, for pity's sake," Ser Gentile mumbled. "Tell him we will be there in two hours."

The boy nodded. With one more obnoxious glance at my somewhat soiled attire, he departed.

"Why in the devil does he want you to come?" the Ser asked, turning a questioning eye to me.

I hoped he did not expect an answer, for I had none to give. In my deluded state, though, I imagined the doge begging Gentile to release me from my meager services as an errand boy to the artist and allow him to install me as his personal companion.

Signora Bellini buzzed around like a bee at a flower as we made our preparations. This was her usual nature, especially when concerned with the recognition of her sons. An invitation by the doge himself was enough to warm her motherly heart to the very roots.

"Now, Nico, remember your place," she warned me, wiping my face for the third time.

"Mother, leave the boy alone." Giovanni laughed. "This is not his first time in the palazzo. He knows how to behave."

Our arrival at the Ducal Palace was much as it had been other days, only this time our escort ushered us into the *Sala del Maggiore Consiglio*, the main council room. Members of the Great Council stood around. Doge Mocenigo and the Council of Ten sat on the dais.

"Ser Bellini, so good to see you." The doge smiled from his platform. He was a different man to me now, so imposing and almost royal. Not the friendly, elderly confidante I had met in the small chamber, but a figure of power and importance far above me. I stood in the master's shadow, moving back a bit; my knees shook as if they knew something I did not.

"The honor is mine, Serene Prince," Ser Gentile said, but I knew he did not believe it. He rolled his eyes at the interruption to his day. "How can I be of further service to you?"

"We have recently signed a peace treaty with the infidel Sultan Mehmet of Constantinople. His hordes threatened the Levant and further up the coast. It was distasteful but necessary for us to capitulate to him. In any case, to help decrease his thirst for Venice, we have agreed to certain concessions.

Apparently, he is a great admirer of Venetian portraiture. He has requested you travel to Constantinople and paint his portrait. I said you would be delighted."

"And if I am not?" Ser Gentile said drily.

"I wrote it into the treaty."

The artist sighed loudly, but nodded his head. I waited for him to protest, but, true to his nature, painting came first. He muttered under his breath about the light on the Black Sea.

"When shall I go?"

"I have arranged for your passage a week from today."

"Very well. If that is all, I should like to begin my preparations for the journey."

"There is one more thing," the doge said. He tapped his fingers for several moments before he spoke again. "It's about the boy."

"Oh?"

"Nico." He turned to address me. "I hope you can clear something up for me."

"If I may, your honor," I answered. My voice croaked like a frog; I cleared my throat.

"You recall the acorn clasp on my cloak?"

I tried to nod but my neck stiffened, and my shoulders drew up. The artist touched me lightly on the arm. The touch did not lessen my fear, and my knees increased their quaking such that standing was a chore.

"Do you remember seeing it when I gave it to you yesterday?"

"Yes, your honor," I replied, trying to keep my answers steady and clear. "I remember it was on the lapel."

The corner of the ruler's mouth turned down.

"What is this about?" Gentile said sharply, his hand squeezing harder on my shoulder.

"The brooch has gone missing."

"The boy took it." A murmur rose from the group as Foscari strode forward.

I should have known. My legs almost gave out and Ser Gentile grabbed onto my swaying form.

"He has admitted as much," Foscari added with a dismissive flick of his wrist.

"I don't see how," Gentile said.

"I met him coming out of the doge's chamber. The cloak was on the back of a chair. The clasp was not there, I am sure of it. He has already agreed the clasp was there when he was given the cloak."

"It could have fallen off as he walked along," Gentile argued. "There is no evidence he took it."

"A good point," Doge Mocenigo said unhappily.

"I have sent some men to search the boy's things," Foscari said. His tone rang with satisfaction. "If he is innocent, they will find nothing. After all, we want to be sure."

"You did what?" Ser Gentile's voice rose in anger. "You had no right. There is no evidence to support your ridiculous accusation. The lad is honest. He would not steal."

At these words, I shuddered. I *was* honest. But I was also a thief.

"No doubt. But the gold pin is valuable, a rare temptation for a young lad. If the boy were to admit his transgression, the punishment would go lighter on him," Foscari said.

"I did not take it," I protested, but even to myself my statement did not sound convincing.

"You would never steal, I suppose?" Foscari's voice was low and insistent.

I did not answer, for the truth would surely hang me. And the twinkle in Foscari's eye told me he knew this as well. Little investigation would reveal I had a reputation on the street for agile fingers. And despite my innocence, I was sure when the search party returned, they would bring their prize with them.

There was a commotion at the door and several armed guards entered the room, followed by Giovanni Bellini who was shouting and waving his arms, his face beet red with anger.

"This is an abomination," he bellowed. "Gentile, what is the meaning of this?"

"The boy stands accused of thievery," Foscari responded. "Well, what did you find?"

The leader of the guard held up a hand, a small golden acorn between his fingers. "We found it in the boy's apron pocket."

The crowd erupted into an indignant murmuring and I swayed, blackness closing in at the corners of my vision. Cries for justice rose in the air. Both Bellinis reached to steady me, for my face must have been as white as a winter's snow. I had been foolish to think I had escaped the grasp of my enemy. He had me now, a rabbit caught in his snare.

"Take the youngster away. Lock him in the Leads," Foscari said to the guard.

"Wait." Ser Gentile held up a hand. "I want one word with the boy."

Foscari scowled as the Doge nodded.

Both Bellinis knelt before me, and Ser Gentile put his mouth to my ear. "What goes on here, lad?"

"I witnessed him cheating at the election," I said in a whisper.

"Did anyone else see?"

I shook my head. The two brothers exchanged pained glances, and ice prickled in my veins.

"We will do what we can for you, lad," Ser Giovanni said.

"God be with you, Niccòlo," Gentile added.

God's blessing, I thought bitterly as the guard led me from the room. Surely, He had deserted me now. Unbidden, the image of my vanished coin floated before my eyes. The blessings of God were as far from me as the soldo I lost somewhere in the streets of Venice.

SOFIA LISABETTA DI MATTEO DEANDRE

All thoughts fled with her feet. Run, run, run. She had to run to get away from this place. Stop what was happening. Don't be here, don't be in this moment. All is escape. Escape from here.

When Sofia could run no more, she fell, face to the ground. Her thin chest moved up and down, echoing the rhythmic sound of the waves lapping at the docks. She sat on the Molo, tired from her race through the city.

In the water, great galleys floated like mountains rising from a blue field, their masts waggling, chiding fingers against the sunlit sky. As her breath slowed, her eyes stared out over the water. She put her hand in her pocket and touched a small worn object, circular in shape. She pulled it out. The object was wrapped in paper, she opened it. The soldo, almost round, but for one flat side, clipped for use in another coin.

She crumbled the paper in her hand and threw it to the ground, grinding it into the mud with her foot. She held the coin up to the light.

Enough for passage on a boat?

Far in the distance, across the Lido, was the warm wet sound of waves lapping the shore. The sea, the Adriatic, mother to all Venetians.

Mother was calling, and she would go.

CHAPTER 9

Two large guards came up on either side of me and picked me up by the arms, so my feet did not touch the floor. I did not struggle. There was no purpose; I would not win. As they carried me out like a rag doll, the Bellini brothers stood, heads together conferring, the hopelessness of the moment written on their faces.

My captors took me out a small door to the back of the *sala* and we continued down a long staircase. When we reached the bottom, they dropped me, and I fell to my knees.

"Get up and walk, prisoner," one growled. He hoisted me up by the back of my shirt and set me on my feet.

My unsteady limbs moved jerkily forward. In my despair, my body ceased to listen to me, and I must have looked like a drunken sailor as I stumbled forward.

One guard took the lead and the other fell in behind. In this manner, we continued into a small passage, leading me from the palace to the prison.

To get to the prison it was necessary to cross the most famous bridge in Venice. The bridge of sighs. Once crossed, rarely did any return. The echoes of the sighs of many prisoners, seeing Venice for their last time, could still be heard in its very stones.

There were two small, barred windows that faced out towards the lagoon. It was through these openings that prisoners would get their last glimpse of the city. I could not raise my eyes to it, such was my misery.

We arrived in a small antechamber and there the prison master stood ready for us. He was broad in the shoulders and round in the stomach. At his great waist was a ring of keys, which he jingled as we entered.

"Does the prisoner have a sponsor?" he asked the guards as we came to stand before him.

The guard in the lead shrugged his shoulders. "No idea," he answered.

"Another charity case," the man sighed. "Last cell."

The keeper led us down a corridor, on the right side of which were several small cells, and on the left side a stone wall with one window. It was too high and small to see through and gave the only light into the area. We rounded the corner to a last lone cell at the end of the corridor. There were no windows on this side and the darkness was blinding.

Rattling through his keys, the keeper opened the door, and with one rough push, I was inside. The door clanged closed behind me.

Never had a sound been more filled with wretchedness than that clang. I lay where I landed and pressed my face into the dirt floor. Tears, which had not yet come, burst forth from their dam. I cried like a child stripped from its mother's arms. I had not cried since I was a tot, and the sounds that emanated from my core rent the air with their bitter wretchedness.

I lay in my despair for several hours. No one came near me. But even those whose hopes are not more than dust and ashes will, in time, run out of tears. When I had no tears left to shed, I sat up to take stock of my surroundings.

The room was dim and barely seven feet wide. A plaster ceiling hung low over my head, and where it was once white now showed black with mold and dust. Several previous occupants had scratched markings of time keeping or obscenities upon the walls with whatever sharp objects they had obtained. The cell was completely empty, save for a small shelf in an alcove and a bucket for necessaries. Rusty bars closed off the only entry.

I gripped the cool metal, tugging with all my might. Despite the rust, the bars of my cage were as strong as newly forged iron. I leaned my head against them, allowing the coolness of the metal to soothe my raw face, swollen from my tears.

Outside of my confinement, there was a small pile of items. It was impossible in that light to determine what was in the pile, but it looked as abandoned as I. The rattling of metal told me that someone approached. It was the prison master, returned.

"Since there ain't no one to bring you food, you'll get the prison ration. Can someone bring you a bed or blanket?"

I shook my head, moving away from him as he opened the door and threw a small tray on the floor. After depositing the meal, he turned his attention to the abandoned pile and rummaged around in it for a few moments.

"Take that," he said, as he pitched a threadbare, rank mattress into the cell. "I'll see about a blanket."

He clanged the door shut and left me alone in the shadows.

This was the darkest time of my life. In that damp box, I pondered how my destiny had changed. I was no longer an orphan hoping to become a merchant of means and import. I was now a prisoner, hoping not to die.

And yet as I lay there, ignoring the food, curled in a ball, death began to seem like an answer. What had I left to live for?

No one would come to my aid. The Bellinis did not have the means to help. Gentile would leave the city in a week, and soon I would be in the mind of no one. Left to rot in this rat hole. It would be better that I die now. At least I had people on the other side. Perhaps they would put in a good word with the Lord so He would welcome me.

THE FAMILY

The baby cried with gusto as the mother gently bounced it on her hip. At her feet, two small girls, twins perhaps, no more than three. The children clung tightly to their mother's skirts. The mother pushed a stray strand of hair from her forehead, running her hand across the back of her neck. She leaned down to straighten her daughters' hair, her attention diverted as the girl approached them.

"Excuse me, Signora, are you taking this ship?" The girl waved towards the imposing vessel.

The mother looked up, surprised to be addressed by this unknown girl.

"Yes." Her answer was brief. Then she added to the children, "Where is your father?"

"I could help you. With the children."

The woman tilted her head and gave the girl a small smile. "You are taking this trip?"

The girl hesitated. "No, but I wish to travel to Constantinople... I have an uncle. I can pay, I just don't think they will let me on, alone." She held up the soldo to the woman.

The woman's face softened as she hugged her baby close. A young man joined the group. The girl drew back.

"This girl, she wants to help me on the trip with the children," the woman said to her husband.

He shrugged his shoulders. "If you wish, dear," he said, putting a hand on his wife's shoulder. "I don't want you to tire yourself."

The woman smiled. "What is your name?"

The girl hesitated. "Lisabetta," she said. Then, once more, she held out the soldo.

"Keep it, dear. You may need it," the mother said.

Lisabetta slid the soldo back into her pocket.

"Take Lisabetta's hand, darlings."

The tiny children each took one of Lisabetta's hands and smiled up at her as they followed the family towards the waiting ship.

CHAPTER 10

The days were filled with gloom and sorrow. Despite my wish, I could not die. At first, I did not eat; my stomach would not hear of it. The food was easy to ignore, being nothing more than a loaf of hard bread and rusty water. I quickly learned, though, that if I did not eat it, the rats would swarm to it. Not wishing to encounter these uninvited guests, I consumed my unpalatable meals, careful not to leave crumbs to attract more vermin. It was bad enough that the fleas feasted on me daily. My skin blossomed with so many welts and scabs that you could not put a finger on me without touching a wound.

On the third day of my imprisonment, I knew I would not die of misery, for it would have been impossible for me to be any more miserable than I was. The rats might take me, or the lack of food might do me in, but my time waiting for death would not be short.

I occupied myself crying, off and on. Sometimes with loud wailings, sometimes with only soft whimpers. I did not see anyone, save the prison keeper who threw me my daily rations.

The clinking of the keys was my signal that the keeper was coming my way. He stopped in front of my cell and opened the door. He did not have his usual fare with him.

"You're being moved," he said. "Bring that." He pointed to my mattress and blanket. I picked them up in weakened arms and followed him back around the corner of the corridor. We stopped in front of a larger cell near the lone window. He opened it and motioned to me to enter, which I did, my things clutched to my chest.

This new cell was bright compared to my old one. The light from the window reached this area of the prison. And rather than being empty, there was furniture: an armchair, a bed in a small alcove, a table, and a stool. Awed for the moment at this comparative luxury, I failed to notice there was another occupant in the cell until he spoke.

"Do you know where you are?" the man said in heavily accented speech. He sat, one leg crossed over the other, leaning back, his face looking up to the ceiling. His clothes looked fine in the dim light. I could not make out his features.

The door clanged shut again as the keeper locked it and left us alone.

"Does the boy not speak?" he spoke as if almost to himself. "I will try again. Tell me lad, do you know the name for our illustrious abode."

"The Leads," I answered dully, still clutching my filthy mat and blanket.

"Ah, good, he speaks, and rightly, too. Yes, yes, the Leads. Excellent, young lad." He stood up and came into the dull light. "And this is the cell of the great Newcastle, the English adventurer and lover. No doubt you are aware of my daring exploits?"

I was not. But he did not require an answer to the question, assuming the affirmative. His face was round but not full, perhaps because of his imprisonment. His long hair reached his shoulders in dark and bushy waves. Both eyebrows, feminine in their perfect arch, rested high on his forehead.

"The Leads," he continued, as if I was listening as raptly as the most devoted of audiences, "is the most infamous prison in all the world. No one has ever escaped from it. Yet."

I remained silent. Somewhere I had heard the best way to deal with a mad man was to ignore him. When the deranged beggars at San Zulian accosted me, I found it helpful to move on as if they weren't there.

Here my bid for silence was a misstep, as I soon learned; Newcastle loved nothing better than to hear his own voice recounting his many adventures and conquests.

"I am sure you are wondering what such an important person as myself is doing in this putrid place. It is a travesty, of course. The Venetian ladies are spectacular. I behaved in only the most gentlemanly manner to all, but your gracious doge misunderstood most grievously my brief flirtation with his granddaughter. And so, he raised charges of pagan worship against me. As if I had time to practice any religion at all."

He slammed himself back into his chair and for a moment was silent, pondering the injustice of his imprisonment. After his reflection, he spoke again.

"I asked the guard for you to be brought here with me. Don't be embarrassed, but I heard your sorrow, and it touched my soft heart. So, tell me what brings a young whelp, barely wet behind the ears, to this illustrious confinement?"

"I am accused of a crime I did not commit." My voice croaked, as I had not used it—save for crying—for the last three days.

"Yes, yes, I knew it! For what could a lad of your stature do to incur this extreme result?" He waved a hand around at our surroundings and jumped up from his seat, skipping towards me, giggling. He held one hand in the air as if supporting an imaginary platter and the other on his hip. The urge to clap came upon me as he seemed to be in the middle of a theatrical performance.

"I am lucky enough to have friends on the outside who have furnished me with these bare necessities of life. It came into my heart to share my meagre bounty with one who has nothing. You see, I have some influence here in this section of hell. No need to take a knee to thank me." He pointed at the rags I held. "Is that your bed?"

I nodded, thinking it might be better than talking. My heart, which had hung heavy and dead in my chest, gave a faint beat, like a stunned bird coming to life. The devastation which had killed it was being replaced by what? Fear of this mad man? Annoyance at his assumptions of my gratitude?

And yet, I should show gratitude, for though I was still in prison, my outward circumstances were undeniably improved. Yet his demeanor was like that of a mad man, skipping and giggling. Perhaps I would regret being locked in with one such as him.

He came close to me and put his mouth near my ear. "It will be easy to repay my generosity. I have need of your help." He spoke barely above a whisper.

"What do you mean?"

As soon as the words were out of my mouth, I regretted them. I had no wish to listen to the ramblings of this conceited donkey. Yet, as he talked, I admit, there was an undeniable charm in his idiocy.

"Now, where did you say we were?"

"The Leads," I repeated, already regretting my rash decision.

"Yes. The tiptop of the prison wing. Reserved for the most influential of the doge's detained guests. This is how I determined you to be a lad of some note. But, tell me why they call it 'the Leads'." When I did not answer, he continued, "The roof." He pointed up. "We are directly under the roof, made of lead. Scorching in the summer and bitter cold in the winter, a torturous place intended to remind its occupants they must obey the law. And so, we are lucky to be here in early spring, when the temperature is more temperate, but the sun will still be hot enough to broil up there."

"This does not seem much to rejoice over," I said. Truly, I had been so lost in my torment that I paid little heed to the temperature, which I admit was pleasant.

"You are wrong, lad. Quite wrong. Being well learned myself, I have studied the properties of the physical world. I can tell you what I know about this lead. In the heat, lead gets soft." He lowered his voice on the last word and motioned me to draw near. With a furtive glance outside our prison, he reached into his jerkin and pulled out a long, thin metal bar.

"Do you wish to leave this place?"

I stepped back in fear as he held the metal bar high up towards the roof. He meant to dispatch me from this place! I quickly put my hands above my head to ward off his blow.

But instead of coming at me to brain me with the bar, he gesticulated wildly in the air. After a minute, I realized he was using the tool to point to the ceiling.

"If only this were sharp," he mused, contemplating the blunt tip of the bolt.

It took a moment for me to understand. A few more grinning pokes towards the ceiling, and I discovered the path on which he trod. He proposed we cut our way out.

I had little to lose by participating in his wild scheme. As soon as Foscari convinced the council of my guilt, and I knew he would, my life would be forfeit. As a traitor to my city, I would face execution or, worse still, never see Venice again. No greater pain than being considered less than Venetian in my conduct could be inflicted upon me. There was nothing Gentile or Giovanni could do, for Gentile was leaving in only a few days.

Escape was my only hope.

CHAPTER 11

So we hatched our hair-brained scheme.

First, it was necessary to turn our rusted metal bolt into a tool.

"I found this in the pile of the scrabble at the end of the corridor," he smirked. "Laurent is not a wise jailor."

Laurent, the keeper of the prison, was not entirely unkind. He would allow us half an hour a day to walk the corridor, set our faces to look out the window towards the free world outside.

It was on one of these daily walks that Newcastle had come across the bolt. Knowing it would be of use, he had hidden it in his sleeve and then stashed it inside the stuffing of his armchair. It was only recently the idea of sharpening it to create a cutting implement had come to his mind.

I took the bolt from his hand and spat on the end. As he directed, I began to scrape the metal against the rock wall. After several minutes of scratching, small marks marred the side of the bolt, but it had not changed much.

"This will take forever," I said grimly.

"And you have somewhere important you must go? All we have here is time," Newcastle replied.

He had a point, so I continued, and as he predicted,

eventually the side began to flatten. After an hour of work, I ran my finger over the now smoother bolt. The work gave me something to distract my mind. I had no delusions that this plan would work, but the steady motion kept me focused and driven towards a goal.

When I created enough of a flat edge, I turned the bolt slightly and continued the task; in this manner, a point slowly began to emerge.

THE SHARPENING TOOK EIGHT DAYS. Newcastle was no slouch and participated equally in the work. In that time, I became better acquainted with my odd companion. At first, he'd seemed quite unhinged, but I soon discovered that his mannerisms were mostly an affectation to hide the fact that he was very learned and knowledgeable. This was deviously clever, because Laurent was soon convinced that there were very few brain cells between the two of us.

Still, we had to be careful.

When one of us was busy at our task of sharpening, the other took up residence by the door. Newcastle would pull the stool up and pretend to be reading his book in the only light we had. At the first sign of a jingle, he would rap sharply on the metal door and I would dive to insert the contraband back in its hiding place in the chair.

When we had a sufficient point on the bolt, we began to plan our escape.

"We must scrape through the plaster to the tiles above," Newcastle said.

"What will we do with the debris?" I asked. Though it was dim, I doubted large quantities of white powder on the floor would go unnoticed.

He pointed to the toilet bucket in the corner.

We took turns scraping away at the ceiling as we had with the sharpening.

We found the most likely spot in the darkest corner where the light did not shine, hoping the darkness would provide cover for our efforts. The first layer came off easily. As I chipped at it, white powder and small chunks of plaster fell on my head. When I had a hole, I swept up the evidence with a small broom Newcastle fashioned out of a stick and some straw he scrounged from the rummage pile. The powder and chunks were deposited in the waste bucket, and one or the other of us would make sure it was covered.

After a month of chipping, we had a hole big enough to fit my head. We had taken my rat-eared blanket and hung it from the ceiling, putting our bucket behind it to further hide the evidence of our work. When questioned by Laurent, Newcastle was up to the task.

"It is our privy, man. We are not animals." That seemed to satisfy the jailor, and he made no more comment about our hidden corner.

It was a painstaking process, sawing through the tiles and plaster inch by slow inch. Despite Newcastle's assertion the heat would soften the lead, the material still resisted our efforts. A day into the job, my back ached and my neck was stiff.

The hole grew and so did our risk of discovery.

With spring approaching, the flea problem increased. I found sleeping to be difficult, as I spent a good portion of my time slapping away the pesky insects.

Early one morning we were awoken from our sleep by the familiar rattle and clang of the corridor door being unlocked and opened.

"Get up!" Laurent growled, clanging his keys against the

bars of our cell. I sat up and squinted at him. Newcastle groaned in his bed but did not get up.

"Come on," Laurent shouted. "I need you out of there." He opened the door and motioned us out into the corridor.

Finally awake, Newcastle protested. "What is the meaning of this? I don't suppose you are going to let the innocents free?"

"Sweeping for fleas." Laurent answered. There were two servants with brooms at his sides, obviously waiting for us to leave so they might sweep.

My heart plummeted. All they need do was look up and they would discover our hole. I tried to catch Newcastle's eye.

"Fleas?" he said, not looking at me. "What fleas?

Laurent laughed. "Are you mad, man? Just look at the lad's face. This place is infested with them."

He could not deny it.

"Very well," Newcastle said, stretching his arms in the air and yawning. "But I must use the facilities first."

"Can't you wait?" Laurent was in no mood for stalling.

"Oh, if you want a pile out in the hallway to clean up then, yes."

"Fine. Hurry up."

Newcastle completed his task and we both went out into the corridor and the two servants entered our room, brooms in hand.

My legs trembled and I clutched at the wall. My mind screamed, *don't look up, don't look up.*

The cleaners were thorough. They moved the bed and the armchair in order to sweep. As they approached the corner where our work was evident, I began to wonder if I had cleaned sufficiently to avoid suspicion after my last night's work.

"What's all over the floor back here?"

My heart stopped. Our work had been noticed. We were found out.

"What do you mean?" Laurent asked, entering the cell.

"Tis my powder," Newcastle said, with a yawn. "I sprinkle it to cover the odor."

Laurent was standing only a foot away from where the hole was. If he looked up, we would be lost.

"Ye, gods, that stink!" he growled and turned away. "Take that thing out of here." He pointed to the freshly used bucket. The servant took it out, and the other hurried out as well.

I did not breathe again until our cell had been locked with us back inside.

Newcastle convulsed in silent laughter. "Never would I think intestinal difficulties would be my savior," he guffawed, his face red with mirth.

I could not help myself, and I laughed with him.

It took two more weeks to whittle away a hole large enough to fit a man. The cell was swept again each third day, and Newcastle repeated his actions whenever we were invaded. Soon the cleaners just avoided the area, sweeping everywhere else but in our privy.

Each day, I marked a strike on the wall, as many other prisoners had done. The departure of Ser Gentile for Constantinople passed without event in our cage. Any hope of returning to my former way of life faded as time moved on. If it were not for Newcastle and his confidence in our eventual freedom, I would have given up all interest in survival.

We planned our escape for midnight. I lay awake on the bare floor, occasionally batting the rats away with a board I had fashioned for the purpose. The gentleman himself was restless.

"The hour is close, my lad. When we go through, we must not hesitate."

I had grown used to—and even appreciated—my companion's energetic demeanor. Laurent, accustomed to Newcastle's constant prattling, paid little attention to the noises emanating from our cell. We could labor without interruption for long periods of time.

The night of our escape was moonless, as we had hoped. The rain which had so swamped the city earlier in the season had returned, leaving a small puddle forming on the floor under our work. We kept our bucket under the hole and took the opportunity to empty it out the window when we were at liberty to walk the corridor.

The shower was also to our advantage, as it meant no one would be milling about in the courtyard to witness our exit when the time came.

Quiet settled over the Leads; the only sounds were the bodily functions of a few other inmates. Snoring, wheezing, and gas eruptions occasionally punctuated the blanket of silence laying over us.

Little light shone into the room through the opening, as it was only slightly less pitch-black outside than in. Rain beat a frantic drum rhythm onto the tile roof above.

Using some sheets from his bed, Newcastle fashioned a rope and hoisted me up. I pushed my way through the hole, bringing the rope with me.

In minutes, wetness soaked through my thin clothes. The roof was slick with water. Surveying the scene, I quickly found a small smokestack which I tied the rope to, allowing Newcastle to climb out.

In silence we replaced the tiles as best we could, hoping to cover the evidence of our escape.

The job now done; I took a moment to breathe in the soggy air. It was the first free air I had inhaled in many weeks. My lungs thanked me, and my tears mingled with the falling rain. I was free.

CHAPTER 12

Newcastle jostled me and, with his finger to his lips, gave a jerk of his head and began to crawl across the roof. I followed, trying to be silent. He moved with a speed which surprised me, given his age, and I wondered if all his tall tales of heroism might be true. It was difficult to keep one eye on his retreating form and the other on the treacherously wet and slanted roof tiles under my feet.

I missed my footing and slid rapidly down the glistening slope. If I could not stop my descent, death awaited me on the marble courtyard below. For the first time in months, death did not seem a friend.

Panic tightened my chest and I flung out my arms, grasping at the slippery tiles. I fought to gain my hold. My wet and wrinkled fingers grasped at nothing. Kicking wildly, my flattened body slid down the rough tiles, scraping my belly and chest. The edge of the roof neared. Just when I was sure my escape would end broken on the courtyard below, a sharp pain pierced my foot. My flailing limb had found the edge of a broken tile. It sliced neatly through my boot and into soft flesh, halting my fall. A rush of heat and agony exploded through my body and warm liquid filled my boot. I stuffed my hand into my mouth to stop myself from crying out, but it was too late.

Newcastle was upon me in an instant, shushing and murmuring.

"Hurry, lad, what is the problem? We must be silent." There was absolutely no sound of irritation or worry in his voice. Was the man completely inured to danger or just ignorant of it?

"I cut my foot," I answered shortly.

"Bad luck, but no time now to see to it. We are almost at our destination."

Sure enough, our goal, the ballroom gable, was only a few feet away. Why he had chosen this particular escape route, I did not question. I merely followed.

He put an arm around my waist, and together we pressed on to the window. With the deftness of an expert thief, he unlatched it and we climbed in. Inside there was a long drop to the floor. Newcastle went first, tying our makeshift rope to the window ledge. The sheet did not meet the floor, leaving a significant gap at the bottom. But Newcastle did not hesitate. He shimmied down the rope and jumped, landing as lightly as a snowflake coming to rest on the ground. He motioned for me to take my turn, then reached out for me as I jumped.

My injured foot gave way as soon as I landed, but Newcastle steadied me. There was a squelching sound as I hit the ground, and I did not know whether it was from water or blood. I crammed a fist into my mouth once more, to keep from crying out in pain.

We hurried across the ballroom and hid together in a cupboard filled with chairs and candles. Newcastle lit a small candle and bade me take my shoe off.

The skin around the cut had pulled away clear down to the bone, and blood oozed out. My stomach lurched at the sight, and my vision wobbled.

"It needs cleansing and a wrap," Newcastle said, "but I have nothing to clean it with." He tore off a portion of his shirt and bound up the wound.

I placed the foot back in the shoe. The pain was less, but the appendage throbbed with every beat of my heart.

"When we are free of here, you must have the injury seen to. But, lad, what are your plans once we escape?"

The question was a poser. I wanted to put as much distance between myself and Foscari as possible. How to do this, especially now that my running would be slow, I had no idea.

"I suggest looking for the first ship out of here," Newcastle said cheerfully. "Time to see the world, lad, and then you can decide where you want to live the rest of your story."

"I want to spend the rest of my life here," I grunted.

"But surely you realize you cannot."

"What do you mean?" My voice rose an octave.

"We have escaped the Leads, and now will no longer be welcome in Venice. The Council of Ten will never get over the insult." He chortled gleefully.

I remained silent. A new pain, sharper than the one in my foot, had overtaken me.

Newcastle was not completely without sympathy. He read my silence well. "I am sorry, lad; this must distress you. I, too, was banished from my home in England. The queen herself bade me never to show my face in court again. And all because she thought I had...well, never mind what she thought."

"I can't leave Venice," I choked. "I'll sneak back to the cell."

"Nay, you cannot." Newcastle restrained my arm as I tried to rise. His voice was low and gentle. "They will know you aided me, and it will go worse for you. You would not live to see the next sunrise. Try not to fret; there are many wondrous places in the world."

"None like Venice," I said through gritted teeth. The man

was trying to be kind, but the agony in my foot and in my chest wracked me, body and soul.

"None like Venice, but still, like themselves. You will see where this new destiny can take you."

I laughed hollowly. Was this some divine joke? I had asked God to change my destiny, and He had answered my prayer. Rage welled up inside me and spilled out in hot, angry tears. Newcastle averted his eyes, such a gentleman he was, and gave me a moment to collect myself.

"I lost my soldo," I blubbered.

He coughed to cover my shame and, mistaking my meaning, he offered comfort. "No worries, lad, I will gladly supply you with some coin as a repayment for your aid in my daring escape. And when I write my memoirs, I will mention your bravery despite your injury."

The night was growing old. Our escape and journey had taken more time than I would have supposed. We left our closet and quietly made our way to the exit of the palazzo. The doors were barred, as we had anticipated. We hid under a covered table to await the morning when the doors would be unlocked. Our absence would not likely be discovered until late morning when Laurent brought daily rations, but the sheet hanging down in the ball room would raise much suspicion.

I dozed and awoke to Newcastle shaking me gently.

"Here we go, lad, the most dangerous part of our adventure. Try not to limp on your foot. It will be hard, but we must not be noticed."

I nodded and tried to wipe the dirt and tears from my face. I must have looked a sight, for pity reflected in his eyes. He stuck his head out from under the table, noting the coast was clear, and we left our safe harbor.

Boldly, he walked into the corridor, past the sentries on duty, taking no more notice of them than he would a stray cat. I remembered the day I followed another gentleman this closely to enter the Palazzo. The irony of my journey did not escape me. Many times, I had stalked wealthy noblemen like Newcastle, to relieve them of a few coins. It distressed me to think I might have lifted something from this man who had now become my protector.

The guards remained in their places; in fact, they even stood straighter as we passed, recognizing a gentleman's bearing. Newcastle murmured reassurances to me as we walked along, his voice so low only I could hear. He appeared every bit the gentleman, giving instructions to his wayward page.

"Easy as pudding," he purred quietly. "Only a few more steps now. See? There is the door ahead. Out we go, down the stairs and into the piazza."

No one paid us any heed, but my body trembled as our successful escape loomed nearer. The door was only a few feet away, liberty in sight. I could almost feel the sunlight on my face.

"Wait, stop," a sturdy voice called out. My body tensed, and I made to run, but Newcastle grabbed my arm.

"Still lad," he hissed. I tried to calm my sinking stomach. A guard approached rapidly, waving something in the air. Newcastle adjusted his face into a look of annoyance.

"Do you speak to me?" he asked the sentry coldly, even though it was apparent he did. The guard had almost reached us. The open door was mere feet from us. In a quick dash we could be there and out into the piazza and freedom, but Newcastle held me firm. What was the lunatic playing at?

"I beg your pardon, my lord," the guard was beside us now. "But is this yours?" He held something out. It was a hat. Newcastle's hat, in fact. I had not realized it was no longer on his head.

"My goodness." The tone of Newcastle's voice warmed. "My chapeau! Wherever did you find it?"

"By the table, my lord," the man said. "It was on the floor."

The garment in question must have fallen off when Newcastle left our hiding place. I cursed myself for being so absorbed in my self-pity I did not notice the missing hat. It could have cost us our lives.

"For shame, boy," he said, looking at me. "What do I have you for, if not to make sure I am properly attired at all times?" He cuffed the side of my head, but not hard. "Thank you for your attentiveness," he added to the guard. "At least someone is watchful."

He put his hat on his head, grabbed me by the ear and pulled me out the front door and down the steps, scolding me as we went. I hurried along, ignoring the pain shooting through my leg each time my injured foot hit the ground.

As always, the piazza was crowded. We sped across the *piazzetta* and halfway down the Molo in less than a minute. Still, Newcastle rushed us on for quite a while down the Riva degli Schiavoni until we ended up at the far end of the wharf.

There he stopped, leaned against the wall of a nearby building, and laughed. "We just escaped the Leads, the most secure prison in all of Italy, by walking out the front door," he gasped.

I did not join in the laughter. Truthfully, I could not. I felt fully the traitor I was. I had become an enemy of the state I loved.

Newcastle did not seem to notice or care. When he recovered, he stood up straight, adjusted his jerkin, and smiled as if the world was born anew.

"So, lad, where will you go?" He motioned to the row of galleys bobbing like giant sea monsters before us. "India, Greece, Constantinople? Or perhaps you want to search for new lands across the oceans? I, myself, return to England. You are welcome to accompany me, if you wish." He bowed low as if it would be a great honor for me.

"England? I thought the queen banned you from ever returning?" As kind as he had been to me, I still perversely wished to catch him in a lie.

"Oh, she relented," he said, no blush on his face.

"Why?"

"I saved her daughter from pirates off the Dalmatian coast. Queens are fond of their daughters, it seems, and a lot can be forgiven when you aid one. But let us examine your situation. I don't want to be callous, but you must realize our time is short. They will have discovered our disappearance by now, and we'd best be onboard a ship out of here within the hour. You there," he called to a sailor who was preparing the nearest galley for sail, "where is this magnificent vessel going?"

"Constantinople," was the curt reply.

"Ah ha! Did you not say you had a friend, an artist, headed there?"

I remembered my life before prison and before Newcastle had stormed into it. I decided in an instant.

"England or Constantinople, lad?" he prodded gently.

"Constantinople." My voice was hoarse.

"You there, have you a medic on board?" He addressed the sailor once more.

"We do."

"Well, I have a passenger for you. He will require some medical attention. See he gets it."

The captain agreed to take me on as a working guest. True to his word, Newcastle paid for it all. He had many friends and benefactors, this ensured his pockets were always full, even in prison.

"Here we part, lad. It was a pleasure to know you." He

slapped my back repeatedly. "I hope we shall meet again sometime." He tipped his hat one more time and walked on.

"Newcastle," I called after him. He stopped and turned back to me. "The queen really forgave you?"

His mouth formed a mischievous grin. "Yes, lad, she did."

THE COOK

"I will take her." The cook looked Lisabetta up and down in satisfaction.

It was a busy morning at the market, as it always was. The bawling of camels, the haggling of the shopkeepers and the bustle of the crowds made quiet conversation impossible.

"She is so small and delicate," the young mother said to the cook. "But we cannot keep her with us. There is no room at my brother-in-law's house for another."

"Appearances can be deceiving," the cook responded. "It's what's in the heart that counts. Are you willing to work, child?"

"I am," Lisabetta said, pushing her shoulders back. "I am much stronger than I look."

The cook smiled. "She reminds me of myself at that age."

The husband raised an eyebrow, taking in the enormous bulk of the cook, but said nothing.

The mother sighed once more. Then, impulsively, she hugged the girl. "God bless you, child." A small tear gathered on her cheek.

"Please, take this," Lisabetta said, holding out the coin to the mother.

The woman shook her head.

"Put your coin away, child," the cook said in a brisk voice. "There are thieves and brigands all over this marketplace." Warmth grew in her chest as she watched the child slip the coin back into her pocket. She knew she had done a good thing. And therefore, good would follow.

CHAPTER 13

My mind was a jumbled mess of sorrowful thoughts as we pulled away from the shores of Venice, the red gold Lion of St. Mark flag snapping cheerfully in the breeze. How could it wave so merrily when my world might never know joy again?

Our vessel, the Zara, creaked and groaned under the influence of the efficient mariners whose strong backs and muscled arms hastened our departure. I stood on the deck, watching the Most Serene Republic fade in the distance. The air blurred around her as the noises of a bustling city faded, and peace as gentle as a dove settled over us.

I put my hand to my cheek. It was wet. The salty wind cooled my burning face and dried my tears, but the heat in my chest flamed on.

The galley carried mostly pilgrims on their way to the Holy Land, but the ship's complement included some merchants. I entered the berth which would be my home for the voyage. Travelers of all shapes and sizes filled every inch of space; many sat in close clusters, exchanging news from abroad. I wrinkled my nose involuntarily as the air was replete with the scent of bilge water and human filth.

The captain gave me light ship duties: swabbing the deck, working in the galley, and fetching and carrying for the cooks. At times, I walked back and forth along the benches, bringing water to the oarsmen. The splendid sound of the ocean mixed with the rhythm of the rowing lulled the pain in my chest to a low ache. For though we moved farther and farther from the place of my birth, this was still my home. This ship, these mariners, this route, all contributed to the *Stato de Mare*, the Ocean State, which was Venice.

As arranged, I had leave to visit the ship's surgeon. The doctor hemmed and muttered over my foot, applying foul smelling poultices, and advising me to eat plenty of onions.

"I don't like the look of it," he grumbled. "Keep it clean and stay off of it if you can."

These were impossible orders given the squalid, close living conditions in the berth. There was often rank goo running across the floor of the sleeping quarters. Even in the quietest waters, the ship swayed back and forth ceaselessly. I prided myself that my true sea blood prevailed, and I suffered no ill effects from the motion. But my foot did not improve, and after many days at sea, yellow crust and green ooze caked the edges of my wound, and my leg swelled to twice its normal girth.

Shortly after my injury grew worse, the Adriatic awoke angry. The winds whipped high and the cantankerous queen shrilled and whined around us. I kept my eyes on the sky in a semi-fog, buffeted between nausea and pain.

"You should get below," the first mate told me as I stood rooted to the deck, my hands entwined in a length of rope I had been coiling.

"Is it bad?" I said as I stared at the black swirling mass on the horizon. I had no idea whether it was sea or cloud. The angry grey of the water matched exactly that of the sky, and the line between the two had vanished.

"Worst I've seen yet," he grunted in reply. "It will delay us in arriving at our destination. Our price for risking such a voyage so early in the season."

"If we arrive at all," another crewman muttered as he passed by.

I stumbled my way below, hampered by my bad leg and the increasing motion of the ship. Rolling onto my hammock, I lay there bathed in the sounds of moaning and puking around me.

I could have ignored the abhorrent conditions, but I could no longer deny the pain in my leg. I moaned along with the seasick and frightened. Each jerk and toss of the ship in the waves wrenched me in my birth and sent fiery hot pokers through my wound. I cried out in agony. As my condition grew much worse, the physician moved me to his quarters. As fever took me, I wafted in and out of awareness.

"I hope the lad is tougher than he looks," the medic commented, while I lay white and shaking in his infirmary.

At times I was awake, barely aware of my surroundings, then the edges of my world closed in and blackness overtook me once more. I tossed and turned, waking and falling unconscious, in a pattern that took minutes or hours, I didn't know.

When I was lucid enough to take in my surroundings, the ship was in so much disarray, I thought I had fallen into fevered dreams. In my delusions, Foscari bellowed my name. When I came to, I discerned it was the wind, and it had not yet ceased its assault on our vessel. My caregiver soundly ignored most of my mutterings, occasionally calling for me to quiet down. The pitching of the sea carried me up to the top of the *campanile* in Piazza San Marco and threw me down to the paving stones below. I would come around just before I smashed to the ground, then careen back up again as a fresh wave of nausea overcame me. When the motion was at its worst, I called out to my long-dead mother and cursed my God.

The groaning of the ship was at times like a lullaby and at times like a screeching washerwoman. Nurse Francesca frequently haunted my dreams, alternately rocking me to sleep in her arms and shrieking at me to be less useless in my life.

Despite my curses, God saw me through, though I was unaware of His presence. I survived the journey to Constantinople, which lasted a month longer than was normal. But to me, those were dark hours.

Monsters haunted my sleep.

Pain and fever clouded my waking.

Demons of ill-will marched past my bed, sentencing me to all kinds of tortures and damning my soul for my traitorous actions. I protested loud and long against their accusations, but they kept up their torment. When the boat docked, someone took me from the ship to a place I did not know. I remained insensible for many days.

I awoke in a sun-drenched room, bleary and confused to find the face of Gentile Bellini smiling down on me. At first, I thought I was still in my dreams, but when the vision neither changed to a raging lion, nor faded like a ghost, I believed I saw truth.

"Master?" I croaked.

"'Tis I." Gentile nodded, his smile broadening. "It is good to see you have opted to remain among the living."

"Where am I?"

"Don't speak, you are not yet out of danger. It is best to conserve your strength. You are at *Topkapi*, the home of the most illustrious Sultan Mehmet II."

The room was simple; no doubt this was the servant area. The walls were the color of sand and a low rounded door stood open at the far end. A gentle breeze and exotic scent floated in from outside.

"When a ship came to the harbor carrying a sick boy who

called for me, I had no choice but to investigate," Gentile explained. "The kind Sultan agreed to allow me to bring my wayward servant here for treatment. I told a small fib, saying I had sent for you. When you are well, I will have the story of your arrival. But for now, rest."

CHAPTER 14

There are scores of mysteries in the east. The medics in the Sultan's palace treated me with whatever witchery and physics they had, but it was still many days before the fever left me completely.

One evening I awoke, my skin burning, and my body wet with sweat. My covering lay in a crumpled ball at my feet. I rolled over, a labored groan escaping my lips. As accustomed as I had grown in my life to waking in strange places, for a moment I remained puzzled, then memory flooded in.

The Sultan's Palace. I was bathing in the moist heat of Constantinople.

Though sweat snaked its salty way into my ears, I could detect the noise of running water gurgling faintly in the distance. If only I could get to the cooling sound, I would know some relief. Or perhaps it was a heavenly melody luring me into the next world. I did not care. The throbbing in my leg and the burning of my brow was almost unbearable.

I tumbled out of the bed to the hard ground and, like a wounded dog, pulled myself across the floor, out of the room, and towards the blissful burbling. I passed through a columned archway into a small patio. The noise of water grew louder. The inner courtyard was open to the sky, and the outdoor air was cool on my fiery skin. A silver brightness of moonlight painted the night in cool elusive light, and the sweet scent of jasmine filled my nose. In the pale illumination, I could just make out flowers against the white columns. Many colored mosaics adorned the walls and reflected in the fountain at the middle of the courtyard.

A cascade of crystal liquid bubbled up over a tall marble pedestal and spilled into the pond below. It was easy to move myself across the smooth, slippery pathway to the center oasis. I leaned over the edge of the pool, enjoying the refreshing chill of the stone against my burning flesh. I dipped my fingers in the water, then wiped them against my brow and drifted into fevered delusions. Visions of caped men chasing me through the streets of Venice haunted my dreams. Each time they caught me, the sound of Foscari's demonic laughter drowned out my cries for help.

How long I lay there in my hallucinations, I don't know. But the visions cleared and, in my mind, I found myself in a garden. Two others stood close by, speaking in low voices.

In my dream, I strained, moving closer to make out what they said.

"Your Highness." A voice came out of the fog. At the sound of it, I shrank down below the edge of the marble pool, curling up like a child. "I am honored to be in the illustrious presence of the next emperor of the world."

"Of course you are," the other purred. From my place in the dream, I watched the scene unfold. The back of a turbaned head nodded agreement, and a ring of jewels flashed in the moonlight.

"Is your Highness contented with the work Bellini is doing on your portrait?" The first speaker was as cordial as a summer's day.

"Yes, yes, but my court teems with Venetians. Not at all the plan I have for the future." The Sultan Mehmet II, ruler of Constantinople and onetime enemy of Venice, gave a rumbling belly laugh.

The other simpered in response.

Revulsion swelled inside of me, and I balled my fists tight.

"Indeed, your Highness."

"And this proposal of yours, to put me in the Ducale Palace as more than a guest, what is it?"

"It will take place during the *Bucintoro,* the perfect time."

The Bucintoro, Venice's marriage to the sea. Each spring, the doge rode into the bay on a golden boat to perform the wedding ceremony. A most sacred day and joyful hour for Venetians, and this year, in my banishment, I would miss it.

"Marriage and death together," the Sultan said. "Interesting."

"I shall station archers along the rooftops, perhaps in the campanile. The arrows will fly, and Mocenigo will be dead in an instant."

At these words, I gripped the edge of the fountain and tried to stand. I must stop this at all cost. But in my dream, as often happens, I could not move my body and remained frozen as a statue, even as my insides roiled in despair, sending bile to my throat and blood rushing to my ears.

"And then?"

"The next steps have to play out with caution and restraint. I am sure I have positioned myself well to take over the dogeship. The element of surprise is with us, to our benefit."

"How so?"

"It is simple, Your Highness. I will be prepared for the tragedy, the first voice of reason, the first person to take command, to have all the answers and a plan for the city to overcome this most unexpected setback. The council will acknowledge I am a man who keeps his head amid chaos. It is best to play upon their fears. Fear is a great motivator. They will think I am truly the right person to lead Venice."

The first voice of reason? I knew that voice. My hatred bubbled up with such an intense flame that I was sure my eyes had turned red as a dragon's. This vile villain, the man to whom I owed all my misery, still plagued me, even in my dreams.

"Still, it pains me to do a deal with someone who would betray his state." The Sultan's rich voice became low and menacing.

"I don't betray my state; I aid it. The Council grows too comfortable in their power; the doge does only what they say. His death will show the people how weak and defenseless the Ten truly are." The man's voice rose slightly at this.

"Yes, the Ten have made no less than fifteen attempts to end my life. But I have survived their feeble efforts. And soon the Ten will be out and the One will be in." Sultan Mehmet slapped his hand on his thigh. "I still don't see how this benefits me, Foscari."

With super-human effort, I began to pull myself along the floor, gripping the tiled edge of the fountain to aid my progress. As I stared at my goal, the distance grew and magnified, as if each inch I moved forward added two to the distance I must travel. A tunnel opened before me and elongated even as I stared down its pathway. I would never reach them in time.

"As Your Highness is aware, I am a lover of your fair metropolis. Nowhere on earth does a city of more wealth and grandeur exist. If you have brought such success here, how much more will you do for Venice? I am quite willing to work in unity with your empire. The Pope in Rome has not the best interest of Venice at heart. What better recourse than to become part of your dominion to ensure our futures as rulers of the seas?"

"And yourself?"

"As a confidante of Your Highness, I would be the perfect bridge between our two cultures."

"How do I know you won't succumb to the pressure of the Council of Ten as all others have?"

"I intend to be a new kind of doge. One of power, not a weak puppet moved by the mewling complaints of old men and fools. I would be subject to none except to God. Mine is a noble destiny."

"Indeed," the Sultan said drily. "Provided the plan works, you can count on our support for your dogeship, Lord Foscari. The people will accept your rule more easily than any vassal of mine. But I am watching you."

"As you wish."

"Leave me now. It is late, and I tire of you."

Silence reigned as the sound of footsteps receded. There was a rustle and another taller figure emerged from the greenery.

The Sultan barked a few commands which I did not understand to the newly arrived figure. The two continued to talk. I caught Foscari's name once, but in vain did I try to decipher the conversation. The scene slipped from me as I struggled to remain in the moment. It was vital I find out what the Sultan and his companion were saying. But I drew away, further and further, until blackness enveloped me.

CHAPTER 15

I n the morning I awoke to find my master once again by my
bedside. I tried to make sense of what had happened to me
since I had last seen him. Dream and reality mingled like fresh
and salt water in the lagoon, making it impossible for my story to
come out coherently. My struggle must have shown plainly on
my face, for concern grew in his eyes.

"Nico, the doctor has good news. He believes your wound is
healing. You will be your old self quite soon. We can talk more
then." He patted me in his awkward manner and moved to leave
my side.

But I needed to speak before he left; my fogged brain knew
that much. "Foscari." The word shot out of my mouth as my
mind cleared.

Ser Gentile stopped. "What about him?"

"Ser Foscari, he is here, in the Sultan's court." I did not
know if it was a statement or a query.

Ser Gentile's eyes softened. "No, son," he said gently. "The
councilman is not here, curse his interfering long nose. You need
have no worries; you are safe. Here, in the bosom of infidels, you
have never been safer."

I settled back down as tension slipped from my shoulders. So, it had been a dream. Foscari had wormed his insidious way into even my hallucinations. I lay for a time in my bed, staring at the ceiling, mulling over Ser Gentile's words. I was secure now. Safe.

There was a gentle tap at the door. I made a noise which I hoped sounded like an invitation to enter. It would be the physician who had been in often since my arrival.

But instead of the doctor, a young girl appeared in the doorway. She was so slight I would have sworn a breath of wind could have blown her away. The thinness of her body and face caused her eyes to seem enormous. Her hair, a muddy brown, parted down the middle and pulled severely back, made her features look strained. With her came the exotic scent of mint and spices.

She did not speak but brought forward the tray and set it on the little stool which usually accommodated the rear of my sour-faced doctor. She kept her eyes downcast and made a small shrug with one shoulder in what I assumed was an attempt to invite me to eat the meal. I could not remember the last time solid food had passed my lips. The scents were intoxicating. I recognized some from my frequent wanderings in the Venetian marketplace, but others were beyond my limited knowledge. The smells excited my senses, and I closed my eyelids, breathing them in.

The girl gasped, faintly.

I opened my eyes to reassure her I had not succumbed to my fate. "Please don't distress yourself," I said, not knowing if she understood my words. "I am fine. Thank you for..." My words trailed off as exhaustion crept back in to settle in my mind.

"You're welcome."

The response came so softly that had I not seen the almost

imperceptible movement of her lips, I would not have believed she had spoken. Surprise filled me. Not only were the words uttered in my language, but with a perfect accent.

"You are Venetian?" I demanded.

The girl nodded. The small blue vein in her forehead grew bigger as her eyes widened in alarm. She was apparently as frightened by my sudden recovery as by my previous demise. She picked up the black metal teapot and poured out a stream of steaming green-gold liquid into a tiny cup. Removing the lid from a small bowl, she stepped back and repeated the shoulder movement, then turned and disappeared through the door.

I picked up the tea and sipped. Strong mint flavor filled my mouth and nose, clearing out the last of the cobwebs still lingering in the corners of my head. I picked up the small bowl and scooped the food into my mouth. The rice swam in a reddish-brown sauce dotted with several chunks of meat. It was warm and spicy, and the chewing felt good against my teeth. Although there was only a small amount, I was soon full. Satisfied, I lay back in my bed and slipped into a dreamless sleep.

Over the next few days, the servant girl came once or twice. However, our encounters were never long or involved, and were often interrupted by a visit from Ser Gentile or the doctor.

On the fourth day, I determined to find out more about her. Solid food had renewed my strength, and I was able to get out of bed and walk around the room, however briefly.

When it was close to the usual mealtime, I moved the little stool by the door and sat down, leaning my head against the cold stone wall. I sat there for some time, until the familiar knock sounded, and I called for her to enter.

If my presence on the stool rather than in the bed surprised her, she did not show it. She hesitated only briefly, looking around the room for a place to deposit the tray, which she did, on the unoccupied bed. I stood up and blocked the door. Her face blanched and she turned her head in search of a way past me. Her bottom lip trembled.

Irrationally, I did not like the trembling of that lip, and annoyance snaked its way into my thoughts. I wanted only to talk with her.

"What's your name?" I said more harshly than I had intended.

She took a step back, and her eyes darted around the room. In a tiny voice, she answered, "Lisabetta."

"Why are you here?" Again, my tone was rough.

"To bring your meal," came the whispered response.

I made an angry noise, and she flinched. The motion brought me to my senses. I had no right to treat her in this manner. I regretted my harsh tones. After all, she had done nothing but serve me kindly. I wanted so much to have an encounter with a fellow citizen, especially one close to my age. Fear of losing this made me unreasonable. Perhaps Mother Venice had sent me this piece of home to ease the ache of loss.

At this same moment, my weakened body gave up on me. My legs lost their substance, and I clutched at the wall as I slumped to the floor. Lisabetta rushed over. I put my arm around her slim shoulders as she hoisted me up. There was a surprising strength in her fragile form. She helped me back to the cot where I sank down.

"Thank you," I said.

She nodded, dipping her pale blue lids over those great luminous orbs. The color was an extraordinary shade of amber, verging on gold. My mind idly wondered what pigments an artist would mix to create such a tint. Such familiar thoughts sent a small beam of hope through my discouraged heart.

Lisabetta, once again, turned to leave.

"Wait," I said kindly, regretting my previous cantankerous ways. "I just wanted to know why you are here, why you are in Constantinople."

She trembled and dropped her gaze to the floor, then spun and rushed out of the room.

CHAPTER 16

From then on, I sought to make Lisabetta my friend, and she was just as determined to allow no such thing to happen.

When she brought my meals, she avoided eye contact and set the tray down, rushing out. After several failed attempts to draw her into conversation, I recalled the time I trained a stray kitten I found near the orphanage. To make friends, I tempted it with a morsel of something good, always offering, but never forcing. In this way I gained the kitten's trust until eventually he would accept food from my hand readily. I thought so often of this technique when dealing with Lisabetta, she became as a little kitten to me.

"I'm an orphan," I said one day. "Do you know the Pietá? The orphan hospital? I grew up under the not so tender ministrations of the sisters there."

On another occasion, I offered, "The plague took my parents when I was a baby." To most of these remarks, there was no response, not even a subtle shake of her head. My progress was slow, or maybe even nonexistent, I was never sure.

My body strengthened due to the rich food and care I received. My master appeared often in my chamber to check on my improvement. His concern touched me. I had no means to return his kindness. How I might repay him occupied my mind in those quiet hours of rest.

On one such visit, he offered me a way to pay back some of my debt.

"Nico, is your strength sufficiently recovered to resume your duties?"

"Yes, Ser Bellini," I said eagerly. The small hope planted by Lisabetta's presence bloomed like the first flower of spring; perhaps I could yet be an apprentice and save my disheveled fortunes.

"Good, I am glad. Too many sunrises have passed. I am more than ready to finish this work and to return to hearth and home."

The Sultan was eager to have his portrait done in the western style, but his time was limited. And after a month in Topkapi, Ser Gentile had yet to have one meeting with him. But arrangements were finally made, and the first sitting was scheduled for the following afternoon.

Since my health had improved, it was no longer necessary for Lisabetta to bring a tray to my room. At first, I worried our paths would not cross, but the opposite was, in fact, the case. I had access to much of the servants' area and being the apprentice to the famous artist gave me a slightly elevated status. I ate with the help but had no work to do beyond my duties to the painter. This left me free to join her at her tasks. She did not ask for aid; however, she did not refuse my help when offered.

Each time we met I would continue the retelling of my history. I despaired of breaking through her reserve as there was little response from her to some of my more exciting exploits. When I related the mock trial in which they found me guilty of stealing the doge's golden acorn, I noticed a slight change in her manner. She glanced up at me. The tale was drawing her in.

Sensing I might be reaching her, I exaggerated my discomfort during my imprisonment, enjoying the look of horror on her face.

"But you didn't take the pin?" she asked.

I halted mid-sentence, shocked to hear her speak. Recovering myself, I shook my head. "No, I did not."

"But why did he say you did?"

I had left out my previous encounter with Foscari, describing the lottery as if it had progressed normally. I did not want to utter aloud the secret knowledge, the source of all my bad luck.

"He does not like me," I said.

"But why?"

"Why does the dog hate the cat? Who knows?" I shrugged, diverting the topic from dangerous waters. "My master has asked me to go to the market to purchase some fresh pigments for him. Will you accompany me to show me the way?"

She blushed again, but the corners of her mouth turned up slightly, as if pleased despite her embarrassment. I imagine she had rarely received so genial a request. I wondered, not for the first time, what had led this fragile waif to this foreign realm. For as much as she seemed too delicate, she had survived the perils of sea voyages and somehow secured for herself a pleasant situation in the Sultan's palace no less. The overseer of the staff, a dark, bearded giant of a man, dealt harshly with many people, but her gentle nature brought out the same in him. I waited as she wrestled with my proposal.

"I will have to check with cook."

Cook needed some green herbs, so we went to the market. I had been in the city for over a month, but had not yet been outside the palace facades. The brightness of the sunlight, free from the need to sneak through windows and cracks in the stone walls, shone in blinding splendor. The subtle hues of Venice could not compete in any fair way with the vibrancy of Constantinople. Bright gold and white buildings stood out against a turquoise blue sky. The heat of the air cooked the colors to rich opulent shades, like the amber crust on a newly baked loaf of bread.

The market put me in mind of the *Rialto*, the busiest market in the world. People of all ages, dress, and languages mingled without restraint. I inhaled deeply. A stew of scents fed the senses; fresh flowers and spices blended with the pungent aroma of fish and smoke. Vendors vied with each other for the attention of shoppers, shouting in loud voices the virtues of their wares. As we wound through the jostling crowd, I could almost imagine I was back in Venice. The Bosporus, the river which cuts Constantinople in half, sang a familiar maritime chorus into my longing ear.

We easily attained our goals, Lisabetta procuring a fat bunch of parsley, oregano, and mint, and I making a good bargain on a large chunk of red ochre.

A flash of azure cloth caught my eye.

"You like it?" the silk merchant said.

I stopped and fingered the smooth material appreciatively.

"You purchase it for your sister?" He threw the silk over Lisabetta's head and it cascaded around her shoulders like a brilliant blue waterfall. The color illuminated her delicate skin. There was something new in her appearance and my chest tightened. Her face opened into a warm smile as her eyes caressed the fabric. I wanted nothing more than to buy it for her.

"We have no money," I told the merchant, regret causing my voice to crack.

He regarded us with a look of disappointment and removed the cloth deftly from her head. A monkey scurried over the tops of the tent and snatched it from the merchant's hand. He shook his fist at the creature and lobbed walnuts at the animal in a vain attempt to retrieve his wares. It was comical, and Lisabetta laughed out loud. The change in her appearance was remarkable; her face was no longer thin and pinched, but elegant, sleek like a greyhound poised to run.

"I will never wear silk," she breathed as the laughter faded on her lips.

And so it showed, she was a real person, with hopes and aspirations of her own. I wondered where she would be if fate had dealt her a better hand. Would she be planning for a prosperous future rather than mulling over dreams less than dust? What would be her destiny, here in a foreign country not her own?

This morbid frame of mind served me no purpose. Hoping to make her laugh again, I entertained Lisabetta with tales about those most interesting people we passed on our way back from the market. It was an amusing pastime, as there was all variety of humanity strolling by the stalls. French, Roman, Venetian, Greek...all rubbed shoulders with the inhabitants of Constantinople in their flowing robes and multi-colored turbans. There was no such riot of color in Venice, where the residents most frequently chose black for everyday dress. The abandon in the nature of the Turks was strange and appealing.

"You see him?" I pointed to a roly-poly man with an enormous dark beard and orange turban on his head. "He is cousin to the sultan, but they have banished him from the palace because his farts are atrocious."

Lisabetta laughed. "Nico, you are ridiculous."

"What, you don't believe me? You would never guess how much you find out when you are sick in bed."

We talked as we wandered our way through the dun-colored streets of Constantinople, a city so different from what I knew. Here, land ruled, not water, as in Venice. The sounds of camels and cattle filled the air, drowning out the ocean. The country held a beauty foreign to the sea, and I had never yet appreciated it. But, in the lightness of Lisabetta's laugh, a new horizon opened before me.

By the time we returned to the marbled gates of the palace we were fast friends, Lisabetta, Constantinople, and I.

CHAPTER 17

What my next move would be preyed upon my mind. Soon, Ser Gentile would finish with his painting and would return to Venice. But what would happen to me? The artist and I had yet to speak of this.

"Nico, I have almost completed the sultan's portrait," he said one day as I was carefully washing his brushes. I did not answer. What was there to say? After a pause, he continued, "When we return, we must visit the doge and explain your situation, convince him of your innocence."

"And if he chooses not to believe in it?" I did not look up from my work, but my hands tightened on the now clean brush.

Gentile picked up one of the brushes to inspect, then he laid it down carefully, letting out a long, slow breath.

"Do we not pride our Venetian selves on our justice and our defense of the people?" he asked. "Let us have faith in Venice and in God, Nico; only He knows what plans He has for you."

"Ser Bellini, I have presented myself as a pawn in God's destiny, and this is where destiny led me. Not through my hand, you understand, but through the hand of fate."

"Then what has happened was meant to happen."

My face flushed hot. Although I wished to accept my destiny, I could not find justice in my exile.

I turned from Gentile and gazed out at the courtyard where Lisabetta washed a large pot by the well. Her hair, once limp and muddy, gleamed rich and bright in the sunlight. It occurred to me that since I had been here, not once had I placed a finger into the pocket of anyone but myself.

"Son." Ser Gentile put his palm on my head, interrupting my thoughts. "I will go with you and vouch for you. You will not be alone."

My head warmed at his touch, and for a moment I allowed myself to hope. But when his hand moved, coldness replaced the warmth.

"I'll think about it," I answered him. Satisfied with this response, Ser Gentile busied himself with the paints and brushes. "In the meantime, I would like you to make one more trip to the market for me, Nico. I must restock my supplies before we leave."

LISABETTA and I roamed the crowded streets, kicking up dust as we went. As we wandered along, donkeys brayed, merchants argued with their customers, and the nasal sound of someone singing an eastern chant mingled together. It was a feast for the senses.

I had become adept at haggling with the merchant who sold the artists' pigments. Despite our language barrier, I was always sure I had come out the better. No doubt this is what he wanted me to think.

"Cook has asked me to get some tarragon and turmeric for her," Lisabetta said as she spied a vendor selling fresh green herbs.

I nodded and found a small stoop to sit upon and take in the day. The scorching sun baked everything crisp; even my skin was dried out and parched. It had grown as brown as a raisin, and as rough as dried toast. I did not know how much of this eternal sunlight I could endure. Growing restless, I scanned the bustling crowd for Lisabetta; surely, she had achieved her end and should return soon. A black cloak caught my eye. Heavy wear for this hot climate, but a telltale sign of a Venetian. Beside the cloaked person stood Lisabetta, head bowed as she conversed with him.

I frowned. Who was this man?

Taking the wave of a hand as a dismissal, Lisabetta hurried over to where I waited impatiently. "I am ready to go," she said. "Are you?"

Nodding, I stood up and took her parcels from her.

She dipped her eyes and blushed. "I can carry them."

"Yes," I answered shortly, keeping the packages as we moved along. "Who were you talking to?"

Lisabetta kept pace with me, my limp still hampering my speed. She furrowed her brow and gave a quizzical stare. "The vegetable merchant? I don't know his name."

"No, not him, the other, in the black coat. He was Venetian, was he not?"

"Oh, yes. He's a gentleman who has stayed at the palace."

"What did he want?"

It was Lisabetta's turn to frown. "You're a curious one. He had lost his way and needed directions back. These markets can be like a maze."

I nodded uneasily. "Did he share any news of home?"

"I didn't ask," Lisabetta said primly. "It surprised me he recognized me. I had only waited on him once before."

"He probably remembered you because you spoke his language."

"Yes, whenever we have a Venetian guest, I am chosen to help."

We continued to walk along in silence. Venice dogged my steps. Even here, many thousands of leagues from my home, I could never leave it fully behind. Through my veins ran canal water instead of blood, and my heart pulsed with the Stato de Mare. If I stayed here, it was possible I could remain in the sultan's service. Gentile would vouch for me. I might aid with other guests from Venice, talking to them, making them feel at home as I never could.

"Nico, you have been so quiet this day. Are you unhappy?" Lisabetta asked, taking her packages as we reached the palace.

I shook myself. "I'm sorry. I've been a poor companion today. Seeing a Venetian gentleman at the market made me homesick, I think."

Lisabetta laughed, then covered her mouth. "I did not mean to laugh at your pain. It is just I can't imagine the Lord Foscari making anyone homesick for Venice. He's awful."

"Did you say Foscari?" I asked in a dry, dry voice. The world is a big place, but to me it was smaller than an ant hill.

"Yes." Her eyes widened. "You know of him?"

"How long has he been here?"

"A day or two, why?"

My constricted throat loosened. "Only a day or two? You are sure?"

"Yes. He arrived the day before last. I had to prepare his chamber."

Relief flooded over me. He had only been here two days.

"I remember," Lisabetta continued, "because I was told not to put him in the same room as last time. He complained it was too noisy near the fountain at night."

"Last time?" My throat tightened again.

"Yes, when you were sick. He was here for a week."

I sank to the floor.

"Nico, what's wrong, is your foot hurting you?" Lisabetta cried, rushing to me.

My dream was not a dream at all. And if I did not hurry back to Venice, Foscari, the putrid rat, would succeed in killing the doge.

CHAPTER 18

The next day I told Ser Gentile I would travel back to Venice with him.

"Good news! I will send word to Giovanni to prepare your case. We will say Newcastle led you astray. It is a proper defense. And my family will vouch for your innocence regarding the matter of the brooch. All will be well."

I did not argue with him. It was of little account whether all would be well with me. For if someone did not stop him, Foscari would have the doge killed and become ruler in his stead. It was only a short step from there to domination under the Ottoman Empire. I did not tell Gentile, heeding Captain Zeno's warning of long ago, to remain silent. The knowledge would only put my master's life in danger, as was mine. The only person who could help, who would understand, was the Serene Prince himself. He must be told, and I needed to explain it to him directly. There was no other way.

Lisabetta's reaction to my news surprised me.

"You are leaving me?" Her voice quavered.

My throat constricted at the sorrow in her tone. "I have no choice. It is a matter of life and death." My voice was sullen, but she ignored my mood, perhaps guessing its true purpose.

"Nico, what is going on? You have not been yourself since your fainting spell yesterday. There is something wrong, what is it?"

It irked me to have my reaction to Foscari's presence referred to as a fainting spell. "There is much you don't know about me."

"Then tell me."

Her simple words and open expression nearly undid my resolve to keep all my deadly knowledge to myself. But I couldn't place her in such peril.

"I can't," I said, but in seeing her lips turned down in disappointment, I went on, "I must return to Venice; there is someone who is in grave danger."

"From Lord Foscari? What has he done?"

Lisabetta was astute.

"Nothing, as yet, but he plans to take something which doesn't belong to him. I won't say any more, for it would also put you in jeopardy. But trust me, I must return to Venice."

"I'll miss you." Tears clouded her eyes as she spoke. But what was to be her fate? She had been my constant companion all these weeks, yet it had not occurred to me I would leave her behind. I couldn't. So much had been left already.

"You won't if you come too. You don't belong here."

She did not reply, but her face crumpled under my gaze. I touched her arm gently.

"What's wrong?"

The tears poured down her cheeks, but she did not answer.

"Lisabetta, remember all I have told you? What can you say worse?"

She motioned for me to follow her, and I did as she wished. She led me to the little alcove where her small bed and few belongings lived. Reaching in her apron pocket, she pulled something from inside and held it out to me. I opened my palm and she dropped it there.

It was a soldo, lying warm and solid in my smudged hand. It had been many weeks since I had had any lucre to call my own, and the sensation was a good one.

"I can't take this," I said, handing it back to her.

She shook her head. "I'm not giving it to you." Her voice was so drowned by sorrow, I strained to hear. "This is why I can't go back to Venice."

"What do you mean?"

She would not answer me. I took her chin in my hand and wiped at her tears with the edge of my sleeve. "Lisabetta." I made my voice firm but not angry. "You must confess what this is about. There is nothing you can say that will shock me."

She drew in a trembling breath. "Nico, you are so honorable. I tell you I'm not like you. You would despise me as you do Lord Foscari."

Her words pierced my soul. I was not honorable, nor would I ever compare her to Foscari. I did not know which caused me to feel worse, so I addressed the latter. "There is nothing in you resembling the putrid rat Foscari in any way!" I grabbed her arm. "Nothing, do you hear me?" My ferociousness only made her sob harder. I took in a deep breath and let go of her arm. "Don't cry. Forgive my rudeness. Whatever it is can't be as bad as you think."

"I stole it." Her voice was barely audible.

"Stole it? From whom?" I could not imagine Lisabetta taking anything which was not hers. But, I reminded myself, this thin girl had the courage to bring herself all these leagues from Venice without the help of anyone, something which even I had not done. There were depths to her spirit I did not yet perceive.

"From my mo—" She paused. "From my guardian."

"Tell me," I urged.

She told me of her upbringing at the mercy of a woman who was not her mother. Her hands twisted as she spoke of this person, saying little but showing much. She did not say the woman abused her and took advantage of her, but I knew it to be true all the same. Fear and self-hatred closed like an iron mask over her face as she talked.

A rage built up inside of me. I wanted to steal more than one soldo from that old cow. I wanted to take from her all she had stolen from Lisabetta. And yet, my rage would not help. My rancor against those who had hurt her would not give her the absolution which she so desperately sought.

"Explain again how you came to have her money," I asked.

"She was taking me to the hospital because she could no longer look after me. I was supposed to give it to the nurses for my upkeep. But I ran away."

"You were afraid to go to the hospital?"

"A little."

"What happened next?"

She paused before she continued, and her words came out soft and slow when she finally spoke. "We were on our way to the orphanage. We met a man..."

"She wanted you to go with the man?" My voice was sharp.

Lisabetta nodded, tears again streaming down her face. "I was so frightened. I kept running..."

I was silent, unable to speak. My body shuddered at the fate she had escaped. I remained quiet for some time, while she sat staring at the floor.

"I have tried," she continued, "to give the coin away. But it was no use."

As she spoke, a simple solution occurred to me. Perhaps we could heal her bruised conscience. "You must return to Venice. There you can deliver the coin to Nurse Francesca; I'll take you to her. You were told to take the coin to the nurses, and we shall see you do it."

Lisabetta's sniffles stopped. "You would go with me?"

"Yes. And you need have no fear of the hospital. It is a good place." *Much better than you have ever known,* I thought but did not say. "They will take care of you. I will take care of you."

I, who had never had concern for anyone, was now professing to care for Lisabetta. It was a dangerous promise anyway, for when I returned to Venice, I might not even be able to save myself.

Lisabetta dropped her lids, her countenance turning rosy. "You would take care of me?"

"I have just said so," I retorted, angry because I knew the words were not true.

She looked up at me, face shining, I did not deserve the admiration. I was a thief far greater than Lisabetta.

A thief, and now, a liar.

CHAPTER 19

With the portrait of the sultan finished, we prepared for our return voyage. My soul writhed inside as I could not hurry our departure. My only consolation was Easter being late this year meant the Bucintoro would also be late. The festival was a time all venetians wore proudly, but now dread replaced my usual joy. I didn't know how I would convince the doge to listen. And not just listen, but believe, and *act*.

The fear of unbelief or ridicule gripped my chest like icy fingers.

My previous trip across the sea had been so marred by my illness, I knew little what to expect on the return. The crew said within two weeks, weather permitting, we would reach Venice. This left at least three weeks until the festival. Plenty of time for me to devise a plan. I hoped.

Convincing Ser Bellini to bring Lisabetta was harder than I expected.

"Nico, we can't simply bring the girl back. We know nothing about her," the painter chided me gently when I suggested the matter.

"She is a citizen of Venice, displaced in this foreign land. It would be our Christian duty to restore her to her home, where she can learn the faith."

"It seems to me your Christian duty rears its head far too easily when it is convenient for it to do so," he responded drily.

I bristled at this comment. Did my convictions weigh so lightly on me they seemed false when I presented them? But the truth was I had been suffering from a crisis of faith since I had lost my blessed soldo and my life had turned upside down. Still, I clung to the possibility, even now, all this would work for good. However, I was beginning to doubt the Holy Father would want to bless a thief like me. I had done little in my time but serve my own purposes. In fact, I could not remember a time when my mission was any less than my self-preservation. Even bringing Lisabetta to Venice was more about my need not to lose her than for her sake. It stung to see myself so clearly.

"Ser, my convictions aside, the girl wishes to return home and worship among her own people. Perhaps God put her in our path to accomplish just such a purpose."

"And where will she live when she arrives in Venice?"

"She is an orphan. Nurse Francesca will take her in; none are ever turned away."

"I am just a poor defenseless painter." Ser Gentile laughed, throwing up his hands. "If God wills for the child to return to Venice, it is not for me to say otherwise. But you have full charge of her until she is safely in the capable care of Nurse Francesca. Perhaps having the responsibility of another person on your conscience will strengthen your faith."

If he only knew that I was responsible for a much grander person than Lisabetta, he might not chide me so harshly. I could not tell him, so I accepted the instructions, but not with much grace. I tired of others' judgments upon me.

In a foul mood, I gruffly told Lisabetta she would accompany us home.

"I'm so glad. But you don't look pleased."

"I am pleased," I answered, trying unsuccessfully to rearrange the scowl on my face. "Never mind. Let's make our preparations. We leave in the morning."

Gentile, generous to a fault, paid for Lisabetta's passage and refused anything from her.

"Is there no way I can repay you for your kindness?" she asked him in a deep curtsy.

"You must promise to pray for the soul of our friend Nico," he said, as solemn as a monk.

She took him at his word. "I will, though I would have anyway. Niccolò has a beautiful soul."

I was thoroughly uncomfortable and disgruntled by the obvious misperception of my character by both of my companions.

THE HARBOR in Constantinople teemed with activity. Ship sails fluttered merrily in the stiff breeze. The smell of salt and fish tickled my nose. Rows of fishermen displayed the day's catch, the silver scales of the fish glinting in the sunlight. Men in turbans barked orders to half-clad sailors gleaming with sweat as they hoisted crate after crate high into the air and down into the darkness of a ship's hold. I closed my eyes and was transported to Venice by the smells and sounds faster than the speediest galley could ever travel.

When I opened my eyes again, the foreignness of dress and the brightness of the sun brought me back to the present. But the welcome thought of returning home still lived. This water, which floated these proud beauties in their moorings, lapped also upon the footings of the buildings lining Venice's canals a thousand miles away, and it was about to carry me there.

Lisabetta stayed close to me, cradling her small pack like a newborn babe. Her eyes pressed wide open as she shuffled along. The sights were well worth marking. Each ship's mast pierced the sky with vibrant banners announcing its allegiance, but it was the Golden Lion of St. Mark we sought. Despite the brightness of the sun and the brilliance of the colors surrounding me, this flag shone like a beacon in darkness. A twinge of apprehension pinched me as we pushed our way through the masses, fearful all would rise and conspire to keep me from my lawful place aboard.

Lisabetta's hand wormed into mine. My already warm fingers heated at her touch and sweat moistened my palm. I hoped she would not notice.

As we jostled through the thrumming crowd, there was a palpable sense of relief in my soul as my foot touched the gangplank. It was slow boarding, and ahead of us, dressed in customary black, a young priest stooped in an attitude of prayer, the vibrant energy of the waterfront in stark contrast to his demeanor.

After what seemed like an interminable amount of time, we were aboard. Lisabetta and I had passage among the pilgrims below deck, while Ser Bellini had a modest cabin above. We found our places below and settled our meager belongings.

"Let's watch the embarkation," I said.

We climbed the ladder and emerged from the dankness below into the pale warm day. We searched for a spot and settled ourselves in a narrow corner near the stern of the vessel. Wisely, we stayed out of the way of the mariners whose angry glances told us they would not tolerate us hampering them at their tasks. The sails swelled as the impregnable walls of Constantinople shrank before our eyes.

"Are you glad to see it go?" Lisabetta asked.

"No," I said, surprising even myself. "It was a beautiful city, full of mystery and wisdom. I should like to come back again sometime."

"I wouldn't."

"Why not?"

"It's a good place for someone like you, Nico. But not for someone like me."

"Will Venice be better, for someone like you?"

"Maybe." She put her hand on the wooden railing. "I'm not strong."

"Nonsense. You made it all the way to Constantinople by yourself, and you didn't get sick either." I snorted.

"Do you think I'm strong?" She turned her amber eyes on me.

Anger welled up in me, deep anger, towards a world which used her so poorly and left her damaged. "Yes, I do."

Her mouth curved up at the corners. "You do?"

"Yes, but it isn't so important what I think. We have only to please God; what people think is unimportant." My throat tightened, and I could say no more.

She nodded, but the smile remained on her lips. Perhaps it was easier for her to find approval in the earthly realm, since she had had no exposure to the heavenly one.

She put her small hand in mine, and as we stood together, the great city faded into the distance, just as if it had sunk into the sea.

CHAPTER 20

The sea was rough, even though it was well into spring and good sailing weather. I spent much time sprawled sickly in my hammock, moaning in rhythm with the other poor occupants of the hold. I had never experienced seasickness and wished never to be subjected to it again. I wondered if the memory of my illness on my previous voyage had predisposed my body to such misery. Lisabetta was unaffected by the tossing of the waves and delivered me my small ration of daily fresh water, which soon ceased to be fresh. I refused most solid food, as it was mostly wasted in the pool of muck sloshing around below where I lay.

After five days of stormy seas and slow progress, Ser Gentile took pity on me and took me to his bunk, where I could moan in privacy.

By the sixth day, the waters had calmed, and I was able to eat again. I sat with Lisabetta near the prow of the ship, our favorite place to sit, eating some bits of apple, the only thing my stomach agreed to keep down.

The captain strode onto the deck and waved his hands for attention.

"The storm has left our ship in need of attention," he said, as all eyes fell upon him. "I have instructed the crew to make a stop on the island of Cyprus where we will make repairs. This will delay our return to Venice some."

At news of this distressing report, a herd of angry bees seemed to have taken up residence in my insides. Lisabetta, noting my reaction, touched my arm.

"But how long will we stay?" I asked her, knowing full well she had no answer to this question.

Later, I posed the same question to my master.

"I don't know, I am not a mariner," Ser Gentile responded. "Are you in a rush to get home?"

"Will we be back in time for the Bucintoro?"

"Ah, don't want to miss a good party." He laughed.

I wondered if he even remembered my state of affairs in Venice. He had not mentioned them since our last discussion in Constantinople. I tried to shake the feeling of foreboding possessing me. It did not matter what happened to me, I reminded myself often. I had two tasks to accomplish before I ended up back in the Leads. One was to deliver Lisabetta safely to Nurse Francesca at the Pietá, and the other, to warn Doge Mocenigo. I must not fail. This stop in Cyprus must be short. It was only ten days until the festival. In fair weather we could reach the city in five or six, which meant the delay could be no more than four days. Otherwise, I would have to find another way home.

Queen Catrina Cornaro was a Venetian noblewoman who had come to her position through marriage. The king and their son died, leaving her to rule Cyprus with the indulgence of the Great Council.

The queen, known for her love of the arts, naturally

requested Ser Bellini's presence at the palace the moment she learned he was on the island. The artist made his way to her abode with Lisabetta and me in tow. He said we would be in the way of the vessel's repair work were we left to our own devices. But I thought it might not be his true reason for taking us. He was not a naturally social person, especially with ladies, and we might prove some distraction for him.

A courtier escorted us into the regent's private chamber, where we sat and waited for Her Highness to appear. We had barely settled ourselves in the rather ornate chairs before the door flew open and the queen herself hurried in.

She was no beauty, yet she had a light about her countenance which made you believe she was in fact the most beautiful of women. Thin, arched brows roofed soft brown eyes that were pressed into her face like sweet dates in a pudding. A scarf covered her hair, leaving only a little auburn fringe visible. Atop the scarf, a delicate golden circlet decorated with precious stones of red, blue, and green twinkled as she moved. Pearls and black opals drooped from her earlobes and hung around her neck. The heavy russet fabric of her dress fell in gentle curves over her body, sweeping the floor. All this grandeur was somehow not intimidating.

She smiled at each of us as we bowed. "Ser Bellini, you come to paint me?" she crooned as she held out her hands to him.

Gentile took them and lowered his head. "If I were, I would paint you just as you are right now."

"A gentleman's way of saying no." She laughed. "But I will have my way. All the best painters paint me! I insist on it. But who have you brought with you? A young prince and princess?"

"This is Nico, my apprentice, and Lisabetta, his..." Ser Bellini paused. "His sister. Orphans, I am afraid."

The queen examined both of us with a critical eye. "Tut,

tut, Ser Bellini, you must not try to fool me. These are not sister and brother." She walked over to Lisabetta and put her hand under the girl's chin.

Lisabetta quivered slightly at the touch but held her head high.

"Adorable." The queen's face softened as she continued to examine Lisabetta.

The girl's face reddened, and her gaze fell to the floor.

"You have no family, child?"

Lisabetta shook her head. She trembled. I moved forward and took her hand.

"I am her family now, Your Highness." It was impertinent, but I did not care. I only cared this person was scaring Lisabetta.

But the queen took no offense. "What a wonderful boy! You wish to protect your new sister. Although sister is perhaps not the right word. You look like peasant stock, but you might have some noble blood in you. We are sorry we did not recognize it sooner." She laughed gaily. "But Ser Bellini, you brought these children here to distract us, did you not? You know how we love children, but you cannot do it anymore. We have seen through your trick. Now, let's discuss when you will be ready to paint our portrait."

"Whenever Your Highness is in Venice next, I shall set aside all other projects."

The cheerful look left the queen's face. "We fear it will be much sooner than we should like." Her shoulders sagged a little, losing some of their stiffness.

"Indeed? But why?" Gentile asked.

"I doubt the Council will tolerate our rule here much longer. They keep sending councilors here to check on us. The horrible Foscari stopped here last month to poke his wretched nose into our affairs. As if he knows anything about Cyprus."

"Do you think the Council will relieve you of your reign?"

"Yes, I do." To my great surprise, tears formed in her eyes. "They will have us returned to the *Venetto* and send some politicians to rule our people. And we shall be queen no longer and we must leave our darlings behind."

"Your Highness, I am sorry, I pray it will not come to pass," the Ser said, gently.

The queen wiped her eyes and waved away his sympathy. "Children, would you like to go out and sit in the terrace? You are, no doubt, bored with adult conversation."

We went to a small courtyard outside the queen's chamber, which I surmised was her private garden. I had little knowledge of flowers and shrubbery, for not much grows in cobblestone. The riot and abundance of blooms and greenery festooning the marble courtyard dazzled my senses. Lisabetta floated from one flower to the next like a blue and brown butterfly, touching them with her pale hands and dipping her nose to inhale their fragrant centers. I watched her like an indulgent father and found a bench out of the glaring sun to sit upon.

"Lisabetta, may I tell you something?" I said when she sat next to me.

"What is it?" She was still much distracted by the beauty surrounding us.

"I may have to leave without you."

My statement drove the wonder from her eyes.

"What do you mean?" Her voice was tremulous.

"I have to return to Venice as quickly as possible. I can't afford to wait here until they repair our vessel."

"But it might be ready soon." Lisabetta went back to gently caressing the blooms.

"Yes, but if it is not ready to go tomorrow, I have to find another way home before the festival. Ser Bellini will take care of you in my stead. And when you return to Venice, I will be there to meet you."

Lisabetta nodded and said nothing. Then she put her hand on mine. "This is your destiny, Nico. You will save Venice."

A chill ran through my entire body. I could not imagine how she knew this. And this destiny did not sit so well with me. I regretted the fateful day when I knelt in the basilica, so arrogantly calling upon God to change my destiny. I wished it undone. And yet, even as this thought crossed my mind, I knew it was not true. I could easily stay here and wait for events to unfold without me in them. Yet, at the core of my soul, I was compelled to follow this path opening before me. I would come to the aid of those who needed me because it was in me to do so.

So my prayer was answered.

Resolve filling me up to bursting, I stood, just as a liveried page entered the garden.

"The queen requests your presence."

I offered my hand to Lisabetta, and we walked together, back into the chamber we had quitted a short time ago.

"There they are!" Queen Caterina exclaimed at our reentry. "Child," she began, taking Lisabetta's hand, "it is you who has taken up much of our conversation this past hour. We have convinced Ser Gentile you should remain here with us. Our climate is wonderful, and we would be a loving mother to you. Our own dear son is now among the angels, and though we could not bear another boy around the palace, a girl will soothe our mother's heart. But we would not make you stay without your consent. And eventually you would return to Venice with us."

Lisabetta stood still as a statue. The sound of the birds and wind flowed in from the open window. Time stretched out as neither Lisabetta nor the monarch moved from this posture. Lisabetta seemed like a doll, with no life in her. The queen remained relaxed and waiting, as if she had no other duties than to attend to the whims of this little girl. She had no doubt what Lisabetta would say.

I was not so sure.

It was Ser Gentile who broke the silence. "Lisabetta, Her Majesty awaits an answer." His voice was gentle, prodding, and firm.

As if some fairy had waved a wand over her, my friend came back to life. She blinked her eyes and curtsied low before the monarch. "I'm your humble servant," she said. "My heart will remain with Nico and with Ser Gentile, who has been so kind to me, but God has brought me here for this reason. How else could an orphan girl hold the hand of a queen?"

My happiness sunk low into my bowels. I knew not why I reacted in this manner. I had already determined to leave Lisabetta, and yet, for her to let me go so eagerly stung. In this I was being unfair, but I was not inclined towards fairness. I had been less alone with Lisabetta as my charge. I said nothing, at least having the sense not to make a fool of myself in such noble company.

"Splendid." Queen Caterina laughed. "Then I will send for my lady-in-waiting who will see to your needs." Her eyes swept over Lisabetta's pathetic attire.

A woman entered the room and, at the queen's instruction, led Lisabetta from the hall.

It was all happening so fast, and as she took the woman's hand and departed the chamber, my self-control momentarily betrayed me, and I let out a short cry.

Lisabetta pulled her hand out of the woman's and ran to me. She put her arms around me and laid her head on my shoulder in a quick embrace.

"Nico." Her voice was barely audible. "I, too, must follow the path set out for me. But our paths will cross again."

"You are brave," I said, choking slightly.

She looked into my eyes and, gently, as delicate as a butterfly, she touched my cheek with her lips. It was so fast I did not know it was coming until it was over. Then she grabbed my hand and gave it a squeeze. Letting go, she followed the lady-in-waiting from the room and did not look back.

My throat was tight as I glanced down, she had placed something in my palm. I opened my fingers. There lay her soldo, still warm from her touch.

CHAPTER 21

In the darkness, I left my bed at the inn where Ser Bellini found rooms for us to wait out our stay. I did not intend to remain on this island an hour more than needed. As I scurried down the darkened streets towards the water, neither fear nor worry filled me. I walked the path set before me, and I would continue to do so even should I perish. For this purpose, I was fashioned and allowed to live.

Though it was late, the waterfront was not quiet. Ships came and went at all hours of the day and night. I needed to find one sailing soon. I spied a mariner coiling a rope.

"Does this ship sail for Venice?" I asked him.

"Yes, it do," was his gruff response. "In the morning."

"Can you use an extra hand?'

"See the captain." He shrugged his shoulder and motioned to where, in the dimness, a figure paced back and forth in apparent agitation.

I approached. "Sir, are you in need of help?"

He barely glanced at me. "Do you know how to pull an oar?"

"Yes," I answered with no idea whether or not it was the truth.

"Get on board and find the first mate. We sail as soon as dawn breaks."

The ease with which I had found passage was not surprising. My course was set out before me one stone at a time. I had only to continue stepping.

Had it been light, and the captain been able to see me clearly, I have no doubt he would have laughed at my lofty proclamation. But in my need, the darkness protected me from discovery. Still, as I sat on the benches with the other oarsmen, I looked like a mouse among rats. My neighbor chortled heartily when he saw me, but not unkindly.

"Good luck, lad," he said. "I can sit back and relax wi' the likes of you to pull me oar. I shall have the life of a gen'leman." He laughed uproariously at his own joke, and many of the others joined in.

And, in truth, death seemed a friend when the mighty oar came towards me and the rowing began. But, in time I braced my legs on the bench before me and put my hands on the massive tree trunk and pulled. As I learned the rhythm of the pulling and pushing, the task became manageable, and the crew broke into song to keep the pace up.

When my relief came, my body was no longer my own. As I departed for my allotted rest period, my seat companion slapped me on the back and gave another hearty chuckle, so I supposed I had performed adequately.

Each moment melted torturously into the next. I made small marks on the wall to keep track of the passing days, just as I had done while imprisoned in the Leads. The captain was in as much hurry as I to finish the journey, for though the wind was with us, we did not cease to row. How I managed on my daily portion of black bread and wine, I cannot say, except to suppose some heavenly force sustained me. Men much larger than I fell to the floor when the heat grew unbearable. My only saving grace was cooperative weather, and it spared me the dreaded rocking and swaying of a ship at sea during a storm. I could not have borne more seasickness.

My world had shrunk completely to the backwards and forwards motion of the oar, until my stupor was penetrated by a flurry of activity above deck.

"Landing soon, lad," Horatio, my seat companion throughout the journey, said. I had become a pet among the crew who, when they saw I could work, gave up teasing me. "Will you ever take to sea again after this?"

"I won't," I said through gritted teeth, and pulled all the harder on my charge.

There is something unmistakable about the feel of a ship hitting the dock. And as the bumping motion rocked us, I was out of my seat and up the ladder to the deck in an instant.

Relief filled my chest to near bursting. As I gazed at the city I had long called home, tears fell upon my cheeks. The wind whipped my hair and dried my face. Venice still stood; I had made it in time.

The ship's commander stepped in beside me. "It is a beautiful sight, is it not?" he said, not looking at me but at the buildings crowded together like decorated ladies whispering secrets to each other.

I looked up at him, ready to answer, when the words died on my lips. I knew this man. Captain Zeno, who had pulled me from my prayers and set my feet on a new path.

"A Venetian born and bred?" he asked.

I kept my face averted and my eyes down. It was tempting to lie, but I did not. In a barely audible voice I answered, "Yes, sir."

"This will teach you never to wander from your home again," he said jovially, and strode off, shouting orders to the men on deck.

As soon as the gangplank hit the shore, I made for it, but

before I had gotten far, someone grabbed my shoulder, yanking me to a halt.

"Where are you going, lad?" Horatio asked in his graveled voice. "I know yer anxious to be ashore, but don't leave afore ye get yer wages." He let out another guffaw and manhandled me towards a line where the other oarsmen gathered.

In a moment, I had several coins jingling in my pocket with Lisabetta's soldo.

As MY FOOT hit the stones of Piazza San Marco, my step was light. Yet the hairs on the back of my neck prickled. It would not do to be followed.

I knew where I must go first. Slipping through the crowd I kept a careful eye out, watching to see if anyone fell in behind me. But no one paid head to a thin beggarly-looking boy making his way through the piazza and stealing into the church. I entered the dark interior and sank to my knees behind a pillar; I dared not even take a pew.

My knees grew bruised and my back ached. An hour passed, and I maintained my posture of prayer and waited for guidance.

"Where the devil have you been?" A familiar voice broke through my unspoken prayers.

I opened my eyes.

"I thought you were dead."

A rough shove knocked me from my pose, and I stood, turning to face my old friend.

"Nico, you idiot," Stefano barked, "talk to me."

CHAPTER
22

We hurried out of the church and left the piazza behind, running through the familiar lanes, turning as often as possible.

"Where have you been all this time? Where are we going?" Stefano's questions came fast and furious. I did not answer but kept moving. While Venice is a maze of twisting streets, it is easy to make many turns and end up where you started. Careful to confuse our trail, I turned here and doubled back there.

"Nico, how much farther?" Stefano groaned, his breath coming in quick gasps.

"Not far," I said, as winded as he. I wanted to be sure no one followed us. He gave up his futile attempts at gaining any more response from me and merely jogged in my wake.

When we came to the canal I sought, we slipped into the water. Clinging to the moss-covered walls with crooked fingertips, we inched our way along the side of the buildings. Stefano grunted beside me, making small splashing sounds as we moved.

"When this is over, remind me to pound you," he said, barely above a whisper.

A grin played on my lips. He was a most unlikely angel.

We reached the bottom of a narrow set of stairs leading up to a courtyard accessible only by boat. I pulled myself up out of the water and climbed the wrought-iron gate blocking the entry, Stefano close beside me. Crouching in a corner behind a bush, we shook droplets of moisture from our hair and caught our ragged breath.

"We must talk softly," I said when he seated himself opposite me. The windows in the buildings surrounding us were closed, their colorful shutters barring out the late afternoon heat. "We will hear if a boat approaches."

"Are you going to tell me where you have been? Nurse Francesca was furious when she found out you weren't at the Bellini workshop anymore. Then when she heard you were in the Leads, she was like an angry hawk. She swooped down there the moment she learned what happened."

"Nurse Francesca went to the palazzo?" I was astonished.

"She did. She was told you were dead."

"What?"

"She said they told her another prisoner attacked you. There was blood."

"They all think I'm *dead*?"

"Yes, need I repeat myself? Are you hard of hearing?"

"No one is looking for me?"

"They searched the nearby canal for a body, but they found nothing and gave up. After all, what is the point in seeking a ghost?"

A lightness entered my chest. My untimely demise might just be the fortunate chance I hoped for. If I were dead, no one would look for me. And, until Ser Bellini arrived, no one would know I was not dead. I remembered Gentile's plan to send a message to his brother. Had he done it? Had Giovanni already gone to the palazzo and alerted them to my continued existence? At the moment, there was no way to know.

"Nico." Stefano's sharp voice interrupted my thoughts. "What is going on? You must tell me."

"First, tell me why you are still in the city. Your uncle in Sicily sent for you."

"He did, but he has not arrived to fetch me yet."

"What has taken so long?"

Stefano shrugged at the question. "Who knows? He sent several letters saying he is coming, but much has delayed his departure. The last letter said he would arrive with his family for the festival and take me home after it ended. Nurse Francesca is annoyed about the whole thing."

I remained silent. Poor Stefano, how must he feel with the shadow of leaving Venice hovering around him every day? I owed him something.

"Nico, whatever is going on, whatever trouble you have gotten into, you can count on me."

The heat of shame washed over me at his earnestness. I had always counted myself alone, yet what he said was true. I could trust him. I was not so alone as I had let myself believe. It had been self-indulgent to not acknowledge the many blessings I actually had, right from the start.

I told my friend everything. How Foscari had cheated in the lottery to become a member of the Council of Ten, how I had been chased by thugs, and how Foscari had framed me and sent me to jail. I regaled him with my time in the Leads, wowed him with my escape from prison with Newcastle. This portion of my adventure intrigued him so, he made me relay the details to him twice. I told him of my hideous voyage to Constantinople, of my overhearing of the sultan's plan, and of my return to Venice.

Of Lisabetta, I said nothing. I cannot say why I chose to leave her small part in my adventures a secret. If he suspected anything amiss, he gave no sign.

"If I didn't know you so well, I would indeed imagine you created this tale to fool me. What plans have you now?"

"My only plan is to tell the doge."

"Oh, tell the doge is all? Shall we stroll up to the palazzo door and ask his Serene Highness to take an amble along the Lido with us?"

"I know it seems futile. But I must see him and tell him. I trust no one else. Foscari may have many council members in his purse."

"What about Captain Zeno, the gentleman who took you to the palazzo in the first place? You told him what you had seen."

I paused and mulled over Stefano's words. I wanted to believe the captain would hear me, but I was not convinced. He had done nothing in our previous encounter. I had been put into prison, and no one had come to my aid. I couldn't trust anyone else.

I shook my head. "No, I can't risk it. I must get to the doge on my own and in private."

We sat in silence, both of us lost in our own miserable thoughts. The cooing of pigeons roosting on the rooftops filled the air with a contented sighing. Above us, one of the shuttered windows opened, and someone splashed foul smelling water down into the small courtyard. We pushed back against the wall and held our breaths, but whoever it was did not look out at their handy work and quickly shut the window again.

"Why not get in the same way you got out?" Stefano asked, breaking our long silence.

"What do you mean?" The heat was making me stupid.

"I mean, you cut a hole in the roof to get out, why not go back in the same way?"

I stared at him dumbly. "Preposterous."

"Why? It worked well enough before."

As the idea percolated in my over-heated brain, I saw the

sense in it. Or, perhaps I should say it seemed sensible to me, although it was far from wise.

Stefano, taking my silence as encouragement, babbled on. "I'm sure they repaired the hole you made, but with the right tools, you could easily make another."

"But the escape hole led into the jail cell."

"Yes, but you could make your hole over an open corridor, rather than the cell. Surely you could judge where that would be. When it is dark, we will climb onto the roof and make a new hole, sneak into the palazzo, and find the doge. Child's play. No one expects someone to break *in* to a prison."

"And how will we get onto the roof?"

At this question Stefano laughed loudly.

I pressed my hand over his mouth. "Quiet, idiot!"

He pushed my hand aside and continued to talk in a whispered voice. "Time in the bowels of a ship has addled your brain, Nico. How many times have you scaled the walls of the Pietá to avoid the wrath of Nurse Francesca? Look around you, my friend, all of Venice is connected." Here he threw open his arms and gestured to the surrounding buildings. "All of Venice is connected," he repeated. "By canal or by roof."

My eyes travelled upward where he pointed. There was no denying it. The houses lived shoulder to shoulder, butted up against each other, barely separated by small canals or tiny alleys. It would be easy to find a route.

"Stefano, you are a savant!" I grinned.

He frowned. "Quiet," he said, most sternly, and then laughed himself. "Tonight, we travel the city of Venice like the angels!"

CHAPTER 23

I t was foolish of me to do it, but I could not help myself. Although everyone thought me a ghost, and it was best to remain one, there was something I needed to do before I set out on my venture. In the pale light of dawn, I made my way stealthily into Eglisa San Zulian and hid myself in the confessional. I lingered for some time and had drifted off to sleep when the sound of the confessional window sliding back woke me with a start.

"Yes, my child," the familiar voice of Father Vincenzo murmured in my ear.

I sat up and rubbed my eyes. "Father, are we alone?"

"I believe so."

"No one else is here this morning?"

There was silence for a moment. "I don't think anyone is in the church. Only the Lord will hear your confession."

"I don't fear being heard. It is being *seen* I mustn't risk."

"Oh?"

"Yes, I died some time ago. But I died a thief and am a thief no more. I wish to confess my crimes and repent and begin anew."

"This is a most unusual story."

I slipped out of my side of the confessional and opened the door to where the priest sat.

His eyes opened wide. He reached out his hand, then pulled back.

"I'm not a ghost."

"Nico?" His voice shook. "Nurse Francesca said..."

"Yes, it was a mistake."

The old priest shook his head as if he needed to clear his thoughts. He frowned, his eyebrows coming together as one. "Are you in difficulty, my son?"

"Yes, I am, but I can't tell you all now. It is enough to say I believe I am walking the path God set out for me."

"Good." He nodded, but his face remained troubled.

"Will you bless something for me?" I asked.

"Of course, my son."

It was dim inside the church, but still, I kept as close to the wall as possible. We moved to a quiet corner behind a pillar. Morning sunshine filtered through stained glass, painting red, blue, and yellow splashes on the stone floor.

I reached into my pocket and pulled out the soldo Lisabetta had given me, then handed it to the priest.

He held it up to the sunlight to examine with squinting eyes. "But I already blessed this for you. A blessing does not wear off."

"It's not the same one, Father."

"Ah, your second? You are on your way to creating your fortune, so you can give a larger portion to the church. I only imagined it was the same because of this flat part, here. I saw it on the other as well." He ran his finger around the edge of the soldo and lingered over the flattened side.

I frowned; I had not noticed this before.

Taking a small bucket from the side of the altar, he dipped the money into the vessel.

"*In nomine Patris, et Filii, et Spirtus Sanctum*, Amen," he intoned, making the sign of the cross over the coin three times. He shifted to me and repeated the action. I bowed my head and droplets of holy water landed on me like a delicate rain. With my eyes pressed tightly closed, I could swear feathery wings rustled in my ears. When I opened my eyes, the good priest was staring at me.

"What is it?" I inquired.

But he only rubbed his eyes and peered at me again. He did not answer the question.

"Father, please tell no one you saw me."

"Who would believe me?" he asked, spreading his hands wide. "God go with you, my son."

"He goes before me," I answered, and slipped out into the sunlit campo.

CHAPTER 24

The night breeze cooled my brow as Stefano and I made our way down the empty streets. It was not easy to remain undetected in the city's narrow corridors. The sound easily bounced back and forth between the close buildings, increasing in volume as it went. The cobblestones under our feet did not yield to our footsteps. Fortunately, we had many years of practice slinking past merchants who usually viewed our approach with suspicious glares.

We came to the place Stefano and I determined would be the easiest to climb. I had not realized all my life sneaking in and out of the orphan hospital, avoiding Nurse Francesca's hawk-like eyes and scourging palm, would lead me to this moment. Yet here I stood, ready to scale another wall and enter a jail.

If only I were stealing into my own room and my own cot.

But not tonight, nor would that ever be my path again. For either this venture would succeed, and I could return to my rightful rank as a somewhat insufficient apprentice to a painter, or I would find myself back in a prison cell awaiting the gallows.

The climb was sufficiently easy. This building, like most in the city, had many decorations or missing bricks to create perfect ledges to aid climbers. As fate would have it, the Lion of

St. Mark, the symbol of our great city, graced the corner of the rooftop to which I climbed. I placed my hand into the lion's mouth, pulling myself up on the mighty beast. Level with its face, I stared into its open jaws and breathed in that silent roar of courage. I had come this far, and the lion was with me yet.

It was easy to find the spot of my last escapade, for Newcastle and I had not taken any care to protect the roof tiles as we dug. I calculated from memory the point at which to dig, hoping my recollections were correct.

I did not look down. If I lost my footing, I would meet my end on the stones below and, most likely, take Stefano with me. Tonight, we had only to break through a thin layer of ceiling and our task would be complete.

As I ascended, my thoughts strangely centered on Lisabetta. She was never far from my mind. In my pocket I carried the soldo she had given me, which became my reminder that God conducted my path. I used my remaining earnings to purchase a sharp blade. The knife would help to make the task we had to perform much easier than when Newcastle and I had dug through the roof with a sharpened metal bar.

As we approached our work site on the last night, I held my breath. I lived in fear our project would be detected. Thankfully, my worry was unfounded. The tiles we had carefully replaced to disguise our progress remained undisturbed.

"We will break through tonight," Stefano grunted as he cut away at the stucco ceiling. I had a bucket of fresh plaster which he would use to repair our small hole. Whatever happened, I would not exit this way.

"We must," I agreed. "Tomorrow is too late."

"I want to come with you," he said, for the hundredth time.

We'd repeated this conversation every night since we decided on our plan. We both knew discussion was pointless. He would do as I asked, but he did not mean me to think he would always do so.

We worked diligently in silence for some while, carving a small hole only big enough for me to squeeze through. The work was dusty and slow, made slower by the need for quiet. The familiar sound of snoring rose from the cells beneath. Apparently, the occupants of the Leads had little to disturb their sleep this evening.

"I think we are almost there," Stefano murmured.

We pried our fingers into the cracks and gently pulled back on the plaster. A large chunk gave way and a dark hole appeared. I lay on my stomach and stuck my head in cautiously. It was darker inside, so I waited for my eyes to adjust. As I hoped, below us was the side corridor of the Leads, around the corner and out of direct view of the cells or any guards bothering to patrol the hall.

Stefano put the debris from our travail in a sack he slung over his shoulder, then produced the bucket of mortar we brought. Once I was inside, it would be his job to repair the entry hole.

"Thank goodness you're apprenticed to a painter," he murmured. "I would not have known where to obtain this plaster. Are you ready?"

"I am," I answered curtly. With a quick intake of breath, I carefully lowered myself through the opening. Broken stone edges scraped my skin and cut into my clothing as I squirmed through. I dropped to the floor without a noise and stood completely still. The rhythmic breathing and gentle moaning of the prisoners remained constant. I was undetected.

Stefano stuck his head through and, saying nothing, he

pushed his chin forward at me in silent question. I nodded, and he disappeared for a moment. The piece of ceiling reappeared at an angle, moving its way through the opening. I reached up and grasped it. Stefano's face reemerged in the gap. In the darkness, I could not make out his features. I nodded, hoping he could see.

In a sound barely louder than the whispering coo of sleeping pigeons, he whispered, "Blessings, Nico. I will see you again soon."

The void into the night disappeared. I reached up and replaced the missing pieces wet with plaster. At first, they refused to stick, but I held them up till my arms ached, and eventually they took. As the last ray of moonlight waned, I knew Stefano was completing his work. And now I was alone in the gloom.

My previous time in the Leads gave me an advantage when entering here. I was well versed in the activities of the guards and, since I knew where they were, it was easier to keep my presence a secret.

I inched forward, careful not to make any sound to rouse the sleeping residents. As I approached the thick wooden door leading to the outer corridor, I detected a faint light. No doubt the guard on duty kept his lantern at the ready. My fingers found the iron latch; it was locked.

I peered into the darkness, wondering where to hide myself. Obtaining entrance took up the largest portion of our deliberations. I groaned inwardly. I was just as much a prisoner as I had been those weeks ago. And it was my own doing.

"Lord, your servant needs your help," I muttered under my breath.

No sooner had the words escaped my lips than the most abhorrent noise grew in the darkness. I wondered if some poor soul were being pulled apart on the rack, such was the agony of the cry. From the other side of the door, there was swearing and heavy footsteps approaching. I moved back against the wall, so anyone looking through the small, barred window would not see me. A light appeared at the opening.

"Pipe down in there!" a man bellowed. The bitter, yeasty scent of ale wafted into the hall. Other prisoners began waking and calling out, but the cry continued. There was swearing and then the sound of a key jiggling in the lock. The door opened.

I pressed myself flat against the wall as the door swung towards me. If the massive thing hit me, it would smash my bones to pieces, but it stopped short of where I stood, catching on the uneven stone floor, providing a perfect shield to hide my presence.

Whoever had entered—the night guard, I presumed— stormed angrily into the room.

"Quiet down in here!" he bellowed over the din.

"It is Alessandro; he's having one of his nightmares again," a disembodied voice answered.

"Ah, curse him and his guilty conscience," the sentry responded, banging on the iron bars. "You, pig's body, wake up."

I chanced to peer around the door and could make out the guard's back as he held the lantern high in the air, peering into the cell. God had ordained this moment. It was dark, save for the circle of light surrounding the guard. With a studied speed, I left my hiding spot and exited through the opening.

CHAPTER
25

It was almost pitch dark in the outer corridor, except for a pale, moonish glow throwing a silver patch on the wall. I made it to the bridge between the palazzo and the prison. Rarely, perhaps never, did a prisoner make the journey in this direction. I stopped briefly to gaze through openings in the stonework to the canal below. In the distance, the shape of the church of *San Giorgio Maggiore* loomed against the night sky. Crossing myself, I slipped away from the window and slithered along the darkened hallway.

Small lamps gave off a low light, just enough to illuminate my path. The halls were deserted. I judged the time to be after midnight, the morning of the festival.

Today, Doge Mocenigo would perform the marriage of Venice to the sea, if he were not killed first.

I had only one chance.

My familiarity with the palazzo from Ser Gentile and my frequent visits served me well. I easily found my way through the empty corridors to his chamber, but upon reaching my destination, I paused.

I could not simply walk into the doge's apartment through a locked door. If I knocked, I risked waking more than just the doge. After mulling this dilemma over in my mind, I deemed the only course of action was to wait. I found a small alcove outside the room where I secreted myself behind a marble pedestal. A bust of some noble lord of long ago topped the pillar. I knew not who he was, but at this moment I was grateful for his deeds, whatever they might be.

As I sank to the floor, I leaned my head against the icy wall, exhausted. I had not rested well in several days, as nights were chiefly taken up with carving a hole in the roof of the Leads. My bones were weary and protested my cramped quarters. I struggled to keep awake, pinching myself roughly. But the hours of worry and lack of rest proved too much for me.

When I awoke, I blinked in the brightness. It was not the light of the new day. I had slept far too long, and dawn grew old. In a panic, I peered out from my hiding place. There were people moving about in the corridors. My stomach tightened. I could not remain in my current spot, for I would soon be detected.

Checking carefully, I eased my way out of concealment and walked down the corridor. It was doubtful the doge remained in his chamber at this late morning hour.

His open door showed the room was empty. With a quick glance over my shoulder, I ducked inside. His golden cloak lay on a nearby chair, and hope burned in me. He would not perform the ceremony without it. He would return to dress. I need only wait here.

I searched for an appropriate place to hide while biding my time. A small wardrobe in the corner seemed suitable. Inside, there was enough space among the garments to be fairly comfortable. The closet smelled of mold and old shoes—not the most glamorous of resting places, but it would suffice.

I did not have long to stay in my odorous confines. Soon, I detected muffled voices in the room, but I couldn't make out the words. My plans of speaking with the doge in private lay in ruins, but I could no longer wait for a better opportunity.

Taking a deep breath, I swung open the door and stepped out from my dingy concealment. Several backs faced me. The doge and all his dressers, I supposed.

"Your Grace," I said as I emerged. "I must speak to you of a most urgent matter."

At my words, the chatter among them ceased and, just as a flock of birds changing direction mid-flight, they all turned to stare at me.

"Who the devil is that?" There was a flurry of cloaks, and from the gaggle emerged a figure I knew too well.

Foscari's eyes bulged. If the situation were not so dire, I might have been tempted to laugh. But as it was, all humor had left me and, in its place, terror oozed like the Black Death.

He pointed his bearded chin towards the door, and two overly muscled guards moved to block my escape. The other occupants of the room murmured like fussy hens in a coop shooed from a tasty morsel.

"I know him," one squawked.

"The boy who stole the doge's brooch," another replied angrily.

"Gentlemen, gentlemen." Foscari's voice came soothing, like warm ointment. "We have not time for this; the doge is about to prepare for the ceremony. This ruffian, whoever he is, is obviously an intruder. Be he thief or miscreant, we will deal with him later. You"—Foscari pointed at a guard— "take him to my chambers. I will come presently."

Two men approached me, forcefully grabbing my arms.

My momentary paralysis vanished, and I fought like a wild beast, attempting to wrench free. My efforts amused the two guards, who chuckled as I struggled. If escape was impossible, perhaps I could at least draw attention.

"Let me go! I must see the doge," I yelled, hoping my voice would carry into the corridor or someone in this gaggle of men might not be in Foscari's pay.

"Shut him up," Foscari called sharply, as all turned from me.

A foul-smelling hand clamped over my mouth and nose. I struggled furiously. They carried me from the room and down the hall. My feet kicked wildly in the air. A pained grunt sent a thrill of satisfaction through me as I connected with some part of my captor's body. But my satisfaction was short lived. His fist pressed more tightly against my face, causing airflow to cease altogether. I gnashed my teeth, biting down hard, but the hands did not slacken their grip and breathing became almost impossible.

My chance to connect with the doge vanishing, despair washed over me as cold as frozen rain. I had been so sure a clear path lay before me. I had been foolish.

And now, Venice would pay for my idiocy.

CHAPTER 26

I was carried none too gently by the two oafs out of the room and down the corridor. It was just as well, because I would not have been able to walk with such fear gripping my body.

"Where are you taking me?" I asked, trying to struggle but knowing my attempts were pointless.

We soon reached a part of the palace I was not familiar with. The area was deserted. They opened a wooden door to a small stale room. Inside, I was roughly tied to a chair. I hung my head and closed my eyes in attempt to block out my circumstance.

"Wake up. You'll not get out of trouble that way." The man smacked my face and my eyes flew open as pain radiated out from my cheek, then they turned and left the room.

The grate of a metal bolt being drawn closed echoed in the empty room.

In that small and stifling room, I reached full despair. I called out, but no one heard my cries. The bonds pressed tightly into my flesh, and my struggle to free myself only made painful cuts on my wrists.

Eventually, my voice diminished to a croak, and I gave up yelling. Unshed tears burned in my eyes; I would not allow them to fall. What good would they do except satisfy my enemy? My head hung limply, both from the pain wracking my cheeks and the shame settled within my heart.

The sound of the bolt being drawn back sent a jolt of terror down my spine. I understood then the fear of a fly as the threads surrounding it vibrate with the weight of the spider moving in for the kill.

When the door opened, two new guards entered, and floating in the background behind them, the Reaper, Foscari.

One of the guards stood before me and pulled my head up by the hair. I grimaced but tried not to cry out. With a glance to Foscari, who gave a slight nod, the guard slapped my face. The unshed tears I desperately held back began to drip down my cheeks. The guards kicked my shins and dug their fingers into my back.

I cried out repeatedly for mercy.

"Enough," Foscari finally barked.

The two hulks backed away, leaving me bleary and sore in my captivity. A rush of gratitude was quickly replaced with revulsion. I would not let him take my soul.

He glided over to me and hovered by my chair.

I attempted to spit on him, but my swollen mouth would not work. It was no matter; he understood my intent. His eyes bore into me like nails hammered into a coffin.

Death was in the air.

"Why am I constantly plagued by this vermin?" He rubbed his head. His brow wrinkled up. "Why must I, a man of great importance, deal with someone of less worth than a flea on a dog's backside?"

"It is destined," I rattled, my voice scratchy and raw from my ordeal.

Foscari laughed. "Destined? No, no. I have carefully fashioned my destiny, and there is no room for the likes of you."

He grabbed a handful of my hair and tilted my head back so our faces were only inches apart. His breath was hot and sweet smelling, like wine. "You, prying scum, watching my little switch at the lottery. You, in the palazzo, talking with the doge every day. And this…" He held something close to my face.

At first, I didn't understand what it was. Then, my stomach sank.

My letter, my accusation, the one I had put into the Lion's Mouth months ago.

"Are you surprised to see this?" he asked. "Did you not realize I had you followed? How silly to think a paper so small would be safe from my grasp. Such an effortless task to reach in and pull it out." He crumpled the note and threw it into the fire. "I should have done it before, but I am glad I did not. It was pleasant to show you your labor was fruitless."

He pulled my head back further. Pain jolted through my neck, and his eyes, like razors, pierced my soul.

"For a while, I thought you were dead. When Newcastle escaped and they found traces of blood, I imagined your bloodied body slipping noiselessly into the canal, or lying in a deserted alley, your life ebbing away." His eyes flashed with delight at the idea. "Imagine, if you will, my surprise when I heard of an injured servant, the apprentice of Gentile Bellini, being nursed in the sultan's palace. How could you be still alive and well across the world from Venice?" He yanked up on my hair, hard, then dropped my head completely and strode across the room. The fury of his desires emanated from him, sulfurous fumes of evil deeds.

"Even then, you slipped away before I had a chance to do anything. I cursed your name and vowed I would rid the world of your insignificant presence. Do you think you, an orphan of no importance to anyone, can defy me? You must be mad!"

"A lowly flea can cause the dog to scratch," I said, trying

unsuccessfully to sound strong and defiant to match my words. He was on me in an instant, slapping my face with the back of his fine gentleman's hand.

"Impudent!" he howled, turning on the guards. "Get out. All of you wait outside until I call you."

When they exited, he turned his gaze back to me.

"What do you know?" He had returned to his musing tone. "What could you possibly know?"

"That you cheated for your seat in the election."

"That is not what you are here for, just to say I helped myself to gain the place that I so deserve. No, there is more, and I will find out what it is."

I remained mute, letting fear show on my face. I might convince him to let me go with a beating if he thought I only knew of his trick during the lottery.

"Now you are silent? Speak up."

"There is nothing."

"Do you take me for a fool? You asked to see the doge; you were discovered in his chamber. I would think you a thief if I did not know better. No, there is more, and I must learn what it is."

Again, I did not respond. My hands grew numb from their bindings. I wiggled them to return the blood and sensation.

"All this can be over soon, if you just tell me why you are here. Surely there is something you want, no? Nothing? Then someone you cherish? A loved one you care to protect?"

"I have no family."

"No family? So sad. But you have friends? Wasn't there a young lady looking after you, who nursed you back to health in your illness?"

Lisabetta. How could he know? I tried to keep my face uncomprehending, but my jaw clenched, and his eyes caught the movement.

"Ah. There is a sweet girl…a little sister, or a love, perhaps?"

The words sounded vile on his poisonous tongue, as if by his very uttering of the syllables he had violated the innocence of Lisabetta more than those in her life had yet been able to. I choked on the bile rising in my throat.

"There, you are making yourself sick. You need your little nursemaid? I must send someone to fetch her. Where is she now?"

She was far away, safe from his reach. Wasn't she? My body quivered, and the blood drained from my face. I had scant choice, but it tore me up to utter the words. They came from my mouth like shards of hot glass, burning and cutting my tongue.

"I'll tell you what you want to know."

He smirked, advancing on me.

"Who have you told your lies to?"

"No one."

"Don't continue to lie, or I will do to you whatever it is you imagine I might."

"I'm telling the truth. I have not said anything, to anyone." And then, in a stroke of genius, I determined what I should say. I would travel down a path this charlatan would follow. "I hoped if I spoke to the doge, he would give me some money. It was foolish. I should have come to you in the first place."

It sounded lame to my own ears, yet he accepted it, the taste of a lie suiting his palate. This was an action a man of his character understood.

"It is well you didn't try, for blackmail is deadly. No matter, I see the measure of you, and my actions regarding you are clear to me now."

He said no more, but rapidly darted across the room and exited. I was alone. I scoured my surroundings for an escape. The re-entry of the guards interrupted my brief search. They spoke not a word but, with little gentleness, removed me from the chair and placed a sack over me.

They carried me like a net full of fish. I am sure I did not leave the room the same manner I had entered because there was no sound of a door opening. Instead, there was a loud grating noise, such as metal scraping on rock. A secret exit? Through my burlap prison, flashes of light gleamed. It might have been a candle or torch used to illuminate a darkened passageway. The clomping footsteps of my captors echoed hollowly. I was being taken out through a narrow passage. No doubt we were leaving by some back way out to the canal.

The unmistakable echo of water lapping against brick confirmed my suspicions. I was dumped heavily onto a hard surface, and pain speared me from shoulder to hip. I clamped my teeth together to keep from crying out in agony. My body moved with the familiar rocking motion of a boat.

I struggled against my bonds. The struggle yielded little result except a sharp kick in my ribs.

"He's just a boy," one guard grunted.

"Hold your tongue. Who cares what he is? You're not paid to think, only to get this job done," the other growled.

"Then let's throw him in the canal here."

"And risk his body being found? Don't be daft. We'll take him out past the Lido. There will be so many boats out there today, too many to notice if someone drops a load into the bay."

There was a grunt of agreement and the boat swayed gently. They must have imagined my hearing had been curtailed along with my sight, for they did not try to hide their plans. I contemplated shouting to attract attention, but it would be useless. Nobody would hear my muffled cries amidst the blare of the trumpets and the gaiety of the festival crowd. Even in my prison the sounds overtook my senses. The water was no doubt packed with drunken merrymakers riding anything that would float.

I closed my eyes and pictured the surrounding scene, from the lagoon filled with gondolas and galleys, festooned with ribbons of gold and red, to the air, ripe with the scents of the sea and burning pitch. Costumed players acted out scenes from Venice's past along the docks and onboard floating stages. It was a glorious sight in my mind's eye, and for an instant, I was free of my bonds, an actor in the greatest performance on the ocean.

But as my lids fluttered open, I returned to my captivity. I renewed my struggle and received a blow to the head for it. Stars circled in my vision. The sounds of revelries grew fainter as we moved farther from the shore. My chance for escape faded with each passing second. The splash of oars in water was like the sound of a shovel digging into an open grave.

CHAPTER 27

"Have you stolen your master's pig?" a voice called out.

We kept moving, and the ability to fight seeped slowly from my body. Exhausted from struggling and hoarse from many attempts to call out through the sodden cloth pressed between my teeth, despair grasped me. But at the sound of that question, I renewed my squealing.

"Ignore it," one guard whispered under his breath.

"Hey, you! Do you have a pig trussed up in there?"

"No business of yours. Move on."

"Come now, lads, give over. T'would do my soul well to have a fresh porker aboard for the day when I can't remove the stench of fish from my nostrils."

The boat moved faster as my captors rowed harder. My last chance was slipping away. I gathered a breath and squealed as loud as my constricted lungs would allow me.

"It is a pig! Lorenzo, we must convince these gentlemen to do business with us. We have some fine grog aboard. Come and drink to the health of the doge on this joyous wedding day."

"Leave off, 'tis not for the likes of you," growled one of my guards.

"Whatever has happened to the grand Venetian sense of

commerce? Ah, it's lucre you want, I see. Lorenzo, bring me my purse. We will have a fine pig for the captain on his return to his home soil."

"Keep yer gold."

"This is most unseemly," the jolly voice rejoined. "Toss me a rope. Let me teach this wretched creature the proper meaning of hospitality."

Lorenzo must have complied, for the boat shook as someone jumped aboard. My captors swore, and in their scuffle with the intruder, someone's boot connected with my shin, sending a shockwave of pain up my leg.

My body lifted, then I hit the icy water with a loud splash and terror filled my veins as the beloved lagoon of Venice consumed me. I screamed loudly, but my cry was cut short as the sea closed in around me.

"By all the saints," someone yelled, "that's no pig!"

My ears and mouth filled with water and I sank, struggling in vain against my burlap prison. Horror seized my mind and invisible hands tightened around my chest squeezing the last moments of air from my wretched body.

Time slows as the body prepares to die. My limbs curled up like a child in the womb, as if protecting my inner core could save me from this watery grave. My mouth opened in a silent bubbling scream. The water burbled around my face and up my nose. Each beat of my heart was like a hammer on my chest wall, threatening to break through at each thump. Would that it would just explode and release me from this slow torturous fate.

Dropping through the cold darkness, my lungs screamed with pain and emptied of all air. Life seeped out of my body in a languid way, as if this was all there truly were to it, a final release and then nothing.

God save me!

The nothingness grew and warmed in me a still small

desire for this watery grave. As my spirit settled to its fate, an upward jolt woke my fading consciousness. I knew my erstwhile angel had arrived at last to carry me to the heavenly realm. It was at least preferable to the other option. The motion continued for an age. *It must be far to paradise,* I thought.

A stab of air hit my lungs, and I gagged, then vomited up the contents of my stomach, thus dispelling all thoughts of heaven. Water drained from my ears and shouts of anger filled them, as if a battle were in progress. My trappings were removed, and I came up from the tomb blinking and spluttering in the sunlight.

I was upon the familiar deck of a seaworthy vessel, the center of a curious crowd of onlookers.

"It's a boy," one of the sailors cried. "Those sons of a crippled sow."

"They're getting away!" someone roared.

"Leave them go, we know their faces," another answered ominously.

"Nico!"

Hands pulled me up and slapped me on the back. I found myself amongst my old shipmates. A heavenly joy encompassed me at the sight of those rough and kindly men.

"Glad I got a knife in the ugly brute," one of my rescuers cried.

"Nico, what have you gotten yourself into? You've only been here less than a week and your life is already forfeit?"

How long the cajoling and reunion would have continued I don't know, but my senses returned to me and I had not much time to react.

"Where is the captain? I must see Captain Zeno!" I searched frantically around the deck.

"Get the captain!" The crowd grew still at the sound of a cold and sober voice. The familiar countenance of Horatio, my gruff seatmate, who had been a constant companion throughout the difficult voyage, came into view.

Someone must have complied with Horatio's command, for Captain Zeno emerged from his quarters, a deep scowl on his brow.

"How drunk are you imbeciles?" he shouted. "I said I was not to be disturbed."

I ran to him. My legs were still cramped and stiff from my confinement and this impulsive rush forward sent me sprawling face down before him on the deck. Blood spurted from my nose as it slammed on the wooden floor. I struggled to pull myself onto my knees.

"Who is this?" The captain growled and pointed a long, well-manicured digit in my direction. The contrast between myself and his finger was astounding. I was soaked as a bilge rat, covered in vomit and blood. My clothing was torn, and my hair matted to my head. He raised one eyebrow at my condition and made as if to turn away from me.

"Captain Zeno, it is Nico. I came with you from Cyprus. And I was the lad you chose, in San Marco, the day Doge Mocenigo was elected. The boy whose destiny you changed."

He turned back to confront me, confusion and recognition flitting across his face.

"Sir, we rescued him from two miscreants who meant to drown him," Horatio said. "Why would anyone drown a child? Mayhap you should listen to what he says."

The commander nodded. "What is it, lad?"

"The doge is in tremendous danger; someone is trying to kill him."

A great cry rose from the gathered fellowship. Captain Zeno held up his hands, and the voices silenced. Kneeling, he took a kerchief out of his pocket and wiped my face. His touch was tender, and although the two were not similar, it reminded me of Lisabetta. I blubbered at the remembrance of her care for me. I missed my friend.

"Calm yourself, lad. Tell me everything, and be quick," he said when he had completed his task.

And so, the tale came out. Once a few sentences escaped, it was like the dam breached, and from my lips poured forth a torrent of words. It was as if I were not the one speaking, as if the story begged telling and had taken charge of my senses. Before I finished, the captain rose from his knee and pulled me with him. While I talked, he shouted orders to his company.

"Man the oars, hard to port!"

The crew responded to his barks with lightning speed, but even I knew to turn a boat of this size was no simple task. My eye raked the city, decked in splendor, and my hands gripped the rail as I listened to the groan of the ship as she turned her face to the crowded lagoon.

CHAPTER
28

As I stood gazing across the gondola-filled lagoon to Piazza San Marco, a presentiment set upon me. Gaily festooned boats crowded the waters, brimming over with happy revelers, most of whom had said farewell to their sobriety some hours past. Amidst this joyous spectacle it became clear no ship could navigate the throng with any speed, if at all. I could not stand here and watch what fate might befall my beloved city.

On the forecastle, the bustling crowds of sailors scurried like ants about their business. Their movements were pointless to me. The only necessary actions must occur in the smooth stone courtyard of the piazza.

I did not feel my limbs moving. Perhaps the angel who had dogged my steps from childhood stood behind me, pushing me on. I soon found myself standing by the side of the ship, attempting to undo the knots which held aloft the small craft used for getting ashore in shallow shoals. I fumbled, trying to release the boat from its high peerage, but a pair of far more adept hands took the task from me.

Horatio's skill with the ropes showed him the practiced seaman he was.

"Get in, lad." He motioned to the still suspended vessel.

I complied, jumping upon the railing and into the bottom of the skiff, righting myself quickly. The boat dropped until it hit the water with a bump. I tried to grasp the oars and my hands fumbled, then caught. I turned the nose of the craft towards the shore.

Hoisting himself over the edge with the rope he had untied, Horatio swung himself down beside me. Above, the voices of the other sailors sounded like the distant cry of gulls swooping over the waves.

Horatio steered the little boat skillfully. Regaining control of my body, I joined with him in the rhythmic motion of push and pull, an oarsman's daily bread. We cut through the surf, passing by boats ladened with merry makers. On the breeze, bawdy tunes and raucous laughter filled the air. The shouting of sailors mingled with joyriders, calling out as we rowed by. Some tossed flowers or ribbons in the boat's bottom. Their bright colors and joyful presence were incongruous with our mission. I kicked at them as they floated in the small pool of water gathered there. I was hard pressed not to stop in my task to cast them out.

"Ho, lad." A half-dressed buxom woman hung over the side of a precarious vessel. "Let me show you what your marriage night might be like." Hearty laughter and catcalls rang through the air as we continued by.

Horatio grunted and muttered under his breath.

My back to the shore, I fixed my eyes on the ship we had just left, marking the mast rising over the prow and its slack sails billowing out or sagging down as the wind rose and fell. I knew not what was behind me. In this way, staring and rowing, I prepared for the bump when we hit the bottom stair of the dock. Jumping from my bench, I leapt to the pier and set off at a sprint. It did not take me long to realize I had no idea where to run.

Festival goers spilled from the open doors of the Palazzo Ducal.

"Where is the doge?" I asked a giggling couple who were sharing a drink from the same chalice.

"You have not missed anything," the young woman told me, laughing as she spoke. "The procession from the church is about to start."

The boat used for the parade was docked in its grandeur close to where I stood. It dominated the wharf, a fitting venue for the doge to perform the marriage rite between Venice and the sea. Its arches gleamed yellow in the sun. Across the bow, multicolored flags fluttered gaily in the afternoon breeze. The vulgarity of its ornamentation was an affront to my senses, as it flaunted its riches like an ill-bred aristocrat. Brocade curtains and gold-dipped wood rails were out of place in the normally staid harbor. A few servants milled around onboard, performing last minute tasks, polishing already gleaming surfaces and straightening drapes.

A floating coffin fit for any king.

Its presence by the pier meant he had not yet left land. But any hope burgeoning in me died at the sight of the lagoon. For there were hundreds of merry boats sailing on the green waters, and any of them might conceal a killer.

The sound of trumpets split the air. The crowd moved wavelike towards the center of the piazza where the doge exited the church to a chorus of cheers and cries.

On his head, the silver threads of his *corno* glinted in the sun. He was tall, and his long, flowing white robe made him seem much taller than the councilmen and priests swarming around him in an expanse of black, red, and gold, their faces frozen in expressions of importance or piety.

Beside him, a young boy carried a pillow with the ring he would toss into the sea to affirm Venice's right to proclaim herself the Empire of the Sea. Behind him, the procurators of the *scuole*, schools and charities, walked with somewhat less formality, then came the rest of the Great Council.

I searched among them for Foscari. At first, I detected no sign of him, but then I glimpsed his pointed face near the back of the group. Even at this distance, I could imagine the evil smile playing upon his lips.

I hid behind the ample rear end of a peasant woman who'd had far too much cheer already. The procession approached the Molo, and I scanned the *piazzetta* for any sign of trouble. The throng of tightly packed people created an almost impenetrable wall. I craned my neck and turned my head, casting my sight along the perimeter of the square, wondering where an attacker might be. My eyes came to rest on the *Campanile San Marco*. Towering like a mighty god above the festivities, the bell tower rose tall and sure, a bastion of peace amongst the chaos. From there, I would have a view of everything.

I sprinted towards it, praying the entrance would be unguarded. Questions knocked about in my brain as my feet pounded the hard ground and my body wove through the crowd like a viper through the grass. A shout rang out behind me.

"Boy!"

I did not turn my head.

People crowded the base of the tower, milling about and making merry. I squirmed through the tightly packed bodies. My stomach twisted. A guard leant against the door, his mouth stretched open in a yawn.

My chance arrived almost too quickly for me to take advantage of it. A reveler stumbled into the sentry, falling hard against him. The stench of alcohol on the man was so strong it reached me where I stood. The guard stifled another yawn and pushed the drunkard off with a curse. His attention diverted for but a moment was all I needed. I edged towards the entry leading to the four hundred twenty stairs, which carried bell ringers and librarians to the top of the tower.

No one grabbed me or arrested my progress.

I gripped the handle.

I tugged.

Nothing happened.

I pulled again, and the door swung open.

In an instant, I was inside. I had no time to bring a light with me, and the pitch dark enveloped me. It was impossible to see, as I was still blinded by the brightness of outdoors. I lurched forward until my outstretched hands met cold stone. Stumbling on, I searched for any way up. My eyes made out dim shapes in the gloom. My toe came in painful contact with something, the first stair. As I ascended, the faint echo of footsteps, not my own, reverberated in the tower.

Someone mounted the staircase behind me.

The sound sent icy darts through my blood and cold sweat mingled with the hot already on my brow. Judging by the loud creaks on the steps, my pursuer was large. I increased my pace. My lungs rasped at the stale air, and my legs screamed in protest, but I ignored it all, focusing instead on the dim stairs before me.

Rounding another flight, my boot caught the edge, and I stumbled. My head banged the rail as I tried to right myself. Stars swam before my eyes. I blinked to clear my vision and squinted up. A dim light shone above me. The summit was close. Behind, my pursuer wheezed and cursed. The footsteps stopped as he paused to catch his breath. This sound gave me strength to press forward. Ignoring my ringing ears and sore foot, I climbed in silence towards my goal, not hesitating for pain or breathing.

CHAPTER
29

As I emerged from the dark stairwell, sunlight blazed around me. I was, for a moment, as blind in the light as I had been in the darkened interior. As my eyes adjusted, the great belly of a bell came into sight.

A new plan rocketed through my brain. I had only to find the cord and pull it. Surely the chime ringing out in the middle of the day would signal danger.

I followed the catwalk around the outer edge, holding on to the railing surrounding me on both sides. In the depths of the dark stairwell, I could see no one. The view ahead, of the city, was immense. The Piazza San Marco, the Molo, even the Lido unfolded before me in glorious sunlit splendor. Behind me, the slanting and twisting rooftops stretched out towards the Jewish ghetto and beyond. I crept along the wooden walkway circling the top of the tower. Sticking to the wall and well away from the open abyss in the center, I rounded the third corner, and came to a dead stop.

Someone had climbed here first.

His back was to me, and he leaned out over the brick façade to look down into the activity below. Unaware of my presence, he adjusted his perch, and I froze.

I had found the assassin.

His crossbow stuck out over the ledge as he settled his aim on the procession below.

The crowd parted as the procession of the doge and his companions reached the bucintoro. Once he climbed aboard, he would take himself to the upper level to wave to the people and offer a few words before the boat moved out into the harbor for the ceremony.

Standing there, arms raised, chest open, he would be an easy mark.

A shriek broke from my lips, and I catapulted myself forward at the archer. He had been so absorbed in his task, so unaware of my presence, my cry caused him to jump violently. He teetered above the black hole below. His training served him well, and with little effort, he regained his balance, turning towards me with lightning speed. But I was already upon him. Fighting like a wild cat, clawing and kicking him, a snarl ripped from my chest.

"What the devil," he cried, seizing me. He was strong, and although I was growing closer to manhood, I was no match for him. He picked me up lightly as a rag doll and threw me away from himself. I fell hard on the wooden floorboards, but was up in a moment, renewing my attack.

"I will throw you over, boy," he barked, fighting to regain control of me again.

My arms and legs flailed in a manner which might have been comical, were the situation not so dire. In my desperation, I had forgotten my other pursuer.

Another pair of hands grabbed me from behind. My only hope was to keep them occupied long enough for the doge to be safely out in the lagoon, too far for an arrow to reach.

"Lord God, send your angels now," I prayed under my breath as I was wrenched from the assassin's grasp and dumped once more to the ground. My head spun, and my vision blurred for a moment, as a great hulk leapt over me and joined in the fray. My sight cleared, and I observed my pursuer. It was Horatio, locked in mortal combat with the archer.

"Run, Nico, run," he bellowed.

I leapt up, but not to run. I reached for the bell rope, stretching too far. My balance gave way. I clutched at the cable as my body toppled over into the dark abyss below. Sound exploded around me, and I flew into the air as the massive bell resisted my pull. I held tight, calling upon all the names of the saints I could recall. As the bell swung backward and forward under the burden of my weight, my feet touched something solid, then it moved away again, leaving me floundering in thin air. I was ready for it the next time. I swung back like a pendulum and grasped at the ledge with my toes. Inch by inch, I regained my footing on the rampart and sucked in a huge breath of relief when, once again, I stood on a sturdy platform.

Panting, I continued to pull on the rope. The noise deafened me. I did not know where Horatio and the assailant were. Alone in the dark, the vibrations rang through me as if it were my body clanging from one metal side to the other.

I did not know what happened outside the tower.

Did the ringing of the bells reach the ears of the doge? Would he understand the meaning?

I had lost all sense of time. There was just me, the ringing, and the pulling. I thought this might go on forever.

But my limbs could not hold much longer, and if I lost my footing, I would plummet to my death, shattering the timeless nothing into which I had entered. My fingers began to shake and to loosen their grip. The door burst open and armed guards swarmed in. Powerful hands grabbed me, and I released my grip on the rope, collapsing my full weight into the arms holding me.

The next few moments were a tumult of confusion. A mix

of bodies, swords, and armor whirled in front of my eyes. Shouts and curses competed with the fading vibrations of the great bell as its momentum slowed. I struggled to right myself as I was slung over the shoulder of a large guard. Upside down, I could make out the form of Horatio, sitting on the floor, leaning against the wooden wall of the tower, blood running down his face.

I tried to call to him, but no sound came from my lips. My mouth tasted foul. With one hand I pounded on my captor's back, but my arm held no more strength than a mere babe's, and my efforts made little impression.

"The doge." I forced the word through swollen jaws. My voice sounded faint, but I was so deafened by the bell I may have been shouting. I could not tell.

Nobody answered me or paid me any attention. Words and commands fired around me, but I could make out none of them. My eyes told me the guard was speaking, but only ringing filled my ears even though the bell no longer moved. My arms hung, devoid of feeling and strength. I could no more speak than I could hear.

But I scoured the parapet and, in the distance, Horatio held up a victory fist as he grinned wildly, his face a bloody, triumphant mess.

CHAPTER 30

"Nico, you have truly amazed me," Nurse Francesca said as she cleaned a cut on my lip, none too gently. "I distinctly remember telling you to behave your best, and I cannot understand how one boy can disrupt an entire city."

Back at the Pietá, bloodied and bruised in the company of the doge's guards, Nurse Francesca alternately scolded and coddled me. I tried without success to get them to take me to the Bellinis' workshop, but they did not believe I belonged there.

She shooed my escort away with the promise to return with me to the palazzo the next day.

When morning arrived, Nurse Francesca became a mothering hen. She fixed my hair, fiddled with my shirttails and replaced my bandages. "Stop fidgeting," she commanded as I bristled under these unnecessary attentions. Bad enough having to bathe and put on fresh clothing. All the fussing left me in a foul mood.

"This boy, who rises from the dead, will be the death of me," she murmured as she finished her work. Examining me once more, satisfied, she gave a nod. "If we must return to have an audience with the Most Serene Prince, then I expect you to appear half-decent at least."

As I waited for her to be ready to depart, I peppered her with questions.

"Where is Stefano?" I began.

"Preparing to go to Sicily, to his uncle's." She busied herself tidying up the remains of her doctoring endeavors.

"What? When?"

"Yesterday morning, just before you arrived."

"I have to see him."

"At the moment you have an appointment with Doge Mocenigo. Nico, what have you gotten yourself involved in?"

"Destiny," I answered, tugging at the collar of my shirt. She batted my hand away. "When will he go?"

"Destiny or not, we had best depart. We cannot keep the council waiting."

"But when is Stefano leaving?"

"His uncle said they would board for the mainland this evening."

"Where?"

"Niccolò, enough questions, we have matters to attend to."

We headed towards the Palazzo Ducal. For the moment, I stopped thinking of my friend, as my current situation grew in my mind.

"Will I have to go back to the jail again?"

"Not if there is any justice in Venice." She gazed straight ahead, and her jaw tightened.

"Is there?"

"I believe the good Father would say as long as the heavenly Lord is still here, there is," she said, patting my arm. Although her action was meant to comfort me, its effect was opposite. Nurse Francesca didn't waste time with sentimentality; I never remember her giving a child a hug, as some sisters at the hospital would do. A bad omen to my mind.

We entered the palazzo through the front door and a page

escorted us to the Grand Council chamber. The area was much as I remembered it from my last visit. There was a large crowd filling the room, and we stood warily by the entry, not knowing where to go. Several minutes passed before someone noticed our presence and hurried over. He was tall and dressed in a black cloak, its fabric flowing out as he walked. His hair hung in limp strands by the sides of his face, looking like the remains of a fish dinner were draped over his head.

"Welcome, Signora Francesca. I am Ser Cornaro; I will represent the young lad."

"Is this a trial?" she asked.

"Not exactly, but Captain Zeno requested my presence with the boy as he tells his story."

"Cornaro?" I asked. "Are you related to Her Highness, Queen Caterina?"

"Distantly, yes," he answered, his chest swelling a little. "Now, Niccolò, it's your name? Good, good. The doge will ask you some questions. Answer truthfully and tell everything you know. Can you do it?"

I nodded, trying to ignore his condescending tone. He hurried us towards the podium, and the people parted as we approached.

The dais at the head of the room was fully occupied. We stood in front of that illustrious group. The noise of the crowd hushed as Mocenigo entered to take his seat. He was clad as he had been on those days when Ser Bellini and I had come for his portrait, corno on his head and his brocade gold and red cloak engulfing his body.

"Your Most Serene Prince, we are ready to proceed," Cornaro said.

The tension in the room grew as we waited for the doge to speak. He took his time, touching his fingers together at the tips and pressing them to his lips as if he were deep in thought.

"Now, lad," he said, dropping his hands as he spoke.

I wiped my sweaty hands on my pants and my shoulders tightened.

"There is no need to be fearful." His voice floated into my ears. "You must just tell me the truth. You caused a disturbance in my city yesterday, almost interrupted the marriage ceremony, but fortunately Venice had her bride, and we are yet the Stato de Mare for another year."

There was an amused titter among the attendants.

I raked the faces with my eyes, looking for Foscari.

"Captain Zeno told me you were a member of his crew, correct?"

I nodded.

"He also informed me you fear for my safety. Can you tell me why?"

I nodded again, but before I could answer, another voice rose from the crowd.

"Your Most Serene Prince, do you not recognize this boy?"

"Who speaks?" the doge asked sharply, looking around.

"'Tis I." A tall figure in black emerged from the cluster. The familiar beady eyes and hook nose caused my insides to shake.

"Lord Foscari, what is the meaning of interrupting me?"

"I apologize, Your Sereneness, but this is the thief who stole your golden acorn and went to prison."

Doge Mocenigo widened his eyes in surprise. "Ser Belllini's apprentice? But that boy died at the hands of the miscreant, Newcastle." He looked me up and down. In my current state it was no wonder he did not recognize me. My face, despite the fervent care of my nurse companion, was not its usual shape or color.

"Apparently not," Foscari said, striding forward to stand directly before the platform. "He must have been in league with the villain. You remember, no body was ever found."

The doge frowned and peered around Foscari at me. His brow furrowed. "Send for Bellini. We will have this matter cleared up."

"There is no need to send for my master," I said, finding my voice. "I am the same boy."

"He admits it!" the traitor crowed. "A young scoundrel and an escaped convict. Throw him back in the Leads and let us waste no more of our time here."

"I am a pickpocket. Or, at least, I *was*. But I did not commit the crime I was accused of."

"Silence! You were not asked to speak," Foscari snarled. "This child has stolen precious jewelry, broken out of our prison —where he was rightfully incarcerated—and now he has disrupted our most sacred festival. He has just admitted to being a thief. Why does he still stand here?"

The assembly murmured their assent. They were turning against me, and I had not yet told my story. What would they think of the truth?

"Your Most Serene Prince." Cornaro stepped forward. "May I be permitted to speak?"

The doge frowned and turned his gaze from Foscari. "Lord Cornaro? What have you to say of these events?"

"Captain Zeno sent me to represent the lad."

"This is not a trial, good councilor."

"The captain felt it might be difficult for the boy to speak under the circumstances." He gestured at the formidable assembly.

"Indeed, the child was brought here to tell a story, not to be tried," Nurse Francesca called. "I won't have him bullied. He is in my charge, and we will be heard, or I will take the matter to the procurator."

The men around her grumbled like angry warthogs,

offended that she dared to speak. But she neither backed down nor gave them any notice.

"We were called here for a purpose. Let's accomplish it with expediency. I'm sure your time is most valuable," she addressed Doge Mocenigo, bowing her head.

He smiled and returned her nod. "Indeed, I will tolerate no more interruptions. Cornaro, have the boy say his story and be quick about it."

"Yes, Your Lordship. Nico, please tell us why you rang the bells yesterday."

"I wanted to warn the Serene Prince. His life was in great peril," I answered.

"Why did you feel this to be so?"

"Because I overheard someone plotting to kill him."

A roar went up from the crowd. I don't know if the noise was evidence of shock or disbelief.

The doge held up his hands for quiet. "Proceed," he encouraged me.

"When and where did you hear this?" Cornaro asked.

"I was recently in the court of Sultan Mehmet of Constantinople."

"How did you come to be in Constantinople?"

"It's true I escaped prison with Newcastle. I was not guilty of the crime which landed me there."

"Yet you admitted to being a thief only moments ago." It as the doge who spoke now, interrupting Cornaro's questioning.

"I did, Your Sereneness, and I deeply regret my past life. I would undo it if I could. But my thievery was limited to picking the pockets of gentlemen in the piazza. I would never dishonor Venice by taking anything from you."

"Preposterous! We found the evidence in his very own apron," Foscari blustered again, stepping to the forefront.

"Silence!" roared Doge Mocenigo. "Nico, although you say

you would never dishonor Venice, do you now see you dishonor yourself by your thievery, no matter how small the theft?"

I nodded, eyes on the floor.

"A discussion for another day. I have still no idea why you claim my life is in jeopardy. Please continue your story."

"After we escaped, Newcastle bought me passage aboard a ship bound for Constantinople," I went on, telling Doge Mocenigo of my injury, recovery, and what I had overheard in the garden.

"Did you recognize who was speaking with the sultan?" Cornaro asked when I had finished.

I took a deep breath, letting the air leak slowly out through tense lips. This was the moment which I had been dreading.

"Tell the truth, Nico," Nurse Francesca said, and her words filled me with new determination.

I nodded.

"Who was it?"

No one made a sound. Not a cloak rustled; not a foot tapped.

My mouth was dry, and my teeth ground against each other. Nurse Francesca's jaw tightened, and her nostrils flared in a way I recognized so well. For once I was not the cause of her anger, at least not in the usual sense. Without turning to look at me, yet I knew it was for my benefit, she nodded her head.

My parched mouth moistened, and my lips unlocked. "It was Lord Foscari," I said, loud enough for all the court to hear.

CHAPTER 31

Quiet like a heavy wool blanket remained over the assemblage, as if time had stopped. Then the abrupt sound of a lone person clapping cracked the silence. The noise continued in a slow and methodical beat accompanied by the sharp rap of boots on the tile floor. Lord Foscari walked defiantly back and forth in front of the dais like a pacing lion, clapping and stamping as he went. The man was nothing if not theatrical.

"Bravo, bravo." His eyes shot like arrows around the room, and his mouth pursed in a grimace full of mockery. "Nicely done, young man. A clever ploy. Dear Serene Prince, you might well be advised to take this youth on as an apprentice; his acumen is undeniable."

"Foscari, what do you mean?" The doge showed little sign of love or welcome for this interruption.

"Do you not see, My Prince? What better means to escape punishment than to discredit your accuser? A move worthy of the craftiest lawyer."

"What is your point?"

"My Lord, surely you remember it was I who found the missing brooch on his person. He accuses me in an attempt to expunge his own guilt. No one has ever accused me of wrongdoing. This wicked child seeks to ruin my reputation and make his own. The ploy is obvious. I suggest we waste no more of the council's time and send this criminal back to the jail where he belongs."

My ears barely registered this speech as my eyes fell from his clapping hands to his feet as they stomped their way across the room and came to rest in front of me. The boots were quite worn, cracked and discolored. My gaze locked on them. As he stood before me, his voice washed over me like a cold winter rain, coating my body. But I did not look up; what I saw there on the floor held me more than captive.

"He cannot even meet my eye. Just as well, it is far past time you learned respect for your betters." The boots turned and moved away.

"My Serene Prince," Nurse Francesca said, her voice rising.

"Silence!" The doge's scant patience was worn to a sliver. "Boy, you have made a most grave accusation against a council member. Have you any evidence, save for your word, to show us your story is true?"

"My Prince, surely you will not entertain these ludicrous statements," Foscari stuttered, spittle on his lips. "I cannot stand such lies from the mouth of this...this...nobody."

"I will give you the opportunity to speak. For now, hold your tongue. Boy, can you not look at me and face the one you accuse?"

I lifted my eyes.

"Much better," he said. "It is our practice in Venice to have justice for all, from the most lowly of orphan to the noblest of lords. I intend to understand all in this matter. The very nature and safety of the Stato de Mare, our most revered home, may be at stake. Nico, tell me all you know and no lies. If you lie, you will wish for the comfort of the Leads."

I swallowed hard. Before I spoke, I was struck by the absurdity of the situation in which I found myself. Every nobleman of note in the city waited for my words. How could I, a child of unknown parentage, be the most important citizen of Venice?

And yet I was.

"My Serene Prince," I said, and my voice cracked. Nurse Francesca's hands pressed on my shoulders, and I breathed in, letting air seep into all the corners of my lungs. "This is not the first time I have stood in this illustrious company. Many months ago, I was here, before your election, to assist in the lottery. I observed Lord Foscari in some unusual behavior."

There was a buzz around the room, which grew as I described what had occurred. A murmur of agreement told me some remembered the scene and Foscari's attempt to blame me for his clumsiness.

Perhaps he knew the sentiment of the crowd turned from him, for he remained silent.

"Are you telling me Lord Foscari substituted the ball fairly gained with one he had on himself?" The doge frowned.

"Yes, My Lord." I nodded.

A snort of derision echoed behind me.

"And why would he do this?" he asked, giving the nobleman a look to silence his impatient sputtering.

"I don't know. Perhaps he wished to gain influence over the council."

"And just what would I have done with this extra ball? I am sure you would all agree I could not have magicked it away." Foscari waved his hands in the air dramatically. "I have no skill with sleight of hand."

A laugh rippled through the crowd.

I turned my face towards him. I had to tell my tale. If it was believed, well and good. But if they rejected my story, his demeanor told me I was as good as dead.

"You stepped on it," I answered, looking straight at him, trying not to allow my voice to tremble with the fear I felt.

"Stepped on it? Ha, and I hobbled about with a great big lump on the bottom of my boot for the rest of the day? Did anyone notice my pronounced limp?" There was more laughter as opinion swayed back in his direction.

"You had only to walk but a few steps."

"And what did I do then?"

"You put your foot upon the brazier and allowed the wax to melt into the fire." I clenched my jaw and kept my eyes on him as I uttered the words. Sweat beaded on my upper lip, but I did not wipe it away.

"Well, you are clever," Foscari snarled. "You have come up with a wonderful tale, but again there is no proof of your little yarn. No other person witnessed this fantasy. Is there anyone here who can agree with this story?"

"There is."

A cry from the rear of the room rang out. All heads turned towards the sound of the voice as Captain Zeno strode in. He commanded the attention of the chamber with his masterful posture. He looked every inch the heroic sea captain his reputation afforded him, handsome in his navy trimmed coat, pressed flat with gold buttons up the sleeve. Upon his head he wore the black velvet cap common to all the councilmen, and his hair, as dark as a raven's feathers, flowed long down his back. He removed his gloves as he marched forward, smacking them on his palm as he spoke, as if adding weight to his words.

"My Serene Prince, and fellow councilors, the report you have heard from the lips of this lad is the exact copy of the one he related to me on the day in question."

"This is not proof," Foscari growled, putting his shaking hand behind his back.

"No, you are correct. This is not proof, but confirmation that at least part of the lad's story is true," Zeno responded.

"Why did you not say anything of this matter to anyone?" Doge Mocenigo turned to face the commander.

"In fact, My Lord, I did not think it worthy of mention. I had not witnessed the incident myself, and while the action does not speak well of the character of the man, I did not imagine the offense serious enough to take up the council's time. Foscari was not making any decisions on his own. I trusted most of the members of the council have honest demeanors and would make a wise choice for our next doge."

The doge nodded at this implied compliment.

"I will not stand for these offenses against my character when there is not one shred of evidence beyond the word of this infant these actions ever occurred," Foscari spat, all eyes turned back on him.

"But, My Lord, I have proof," I added, raising my voice above the confusion of chatter.

The doge called for silence yet again, and when order was restored, he bade me to proceed.

"His boot." I pointed to Foscari. "If we were to look at the underside, we should see scorch marks from its proximity to the fire as he melted the wax away. I am sure those are the same he wore that day."

A roar rose around the room. Some cried out in disbelief, some in shock, and some for the sheer joy of it.

"Take off your boots, Foscari," an amused voice called. "Show us the bottom of your footwear."

There was another wave of laughter.

Foscari's face turned as purple as his doublet.

"Do it," said the Most Serene Prince of Venice. "Now."

The rat looked around the room as if he were cornered by a pack of wild dogs. He gurgled and snorted in an affronted manner, sounding like a thick stew boiling over the fire. He did not bend to remove his boot.

"You may do it yourself, or you may have one of my attendants help you," Mocenigo said, gesturing to the guards flanking the dais where he sat.

The villain reluctantly performed the action. Nurse Francesca's hands still rested on my shoulders. To my right, Cornaro, and to my left, Captain Zeno waited. I could practically hear them holding their breath.

Foscari took a sweet long time and, for a moment, I was almost sorry for him as he stood with a bewildered look on his face, examining the bottom of his boot. A gasp escaped the lips of those standing closest to him, and someone grabbed the item from his hand and held it high.

It was there, clearly visible, a round space clearer than the rest surrounded by black scorch marks. Contact with the Venetian cobblestones had scuffed and muddied it, and any physical traces of the wax were long obliterated, but the evidence of the oily mark was obvious to all who stood there, including Foscari himself.

CHAPTER 32

F oscari's protests, though loud and long, were unheeded, for the shoe had convicted him of all counts in the minds of the assembly. But Doge Mocenigo was more astute than the masses. Order restored, and Foscari was held fast in place by the palazzo guard as the hearing of evidence continued.

"While the actions of Ser Foscari are base, and a testament to a lack of honesty in his character, this does not make him guilty of the far more serious crime of which he is accused." Doge Mocenigo's words dispelled the somewhat comical atmosphere fostered by the shoe incident.

The crowd stilled.

My legs ached, my head ached, and my soul ached. I had no desire to continue with this trial, for in my heart I mourned for the loss of Venice's purity. Even for the reprehensible form of Lord Foscari I did not want a conviction, for his guilt would shine a light on my beloved city's flaws. Tears stung my eyes. But I could not recant. I could not.

"The Council will now hear arguments for and against the accused. Bring in the prisoners."

"My Lord, may I have leave to remove this boy? Surely he

can have no more to do with these proceedings." Nurse Francesca's hand still rested on my shoulder.

"Peace, sister. I am afraid your charge might yet have a role to play in these games. But please step to the side. I will call for him if I have need of him again."

As if on cue, the doors were flung open and two guards strode in, pulling with them a pair of disheveled prisoners. The contrast was stark. The first was unknown to me, and I had no inkling who the second poor soul was until he turned his grimy face in my direction. Horatio!

I gasped and made a forward movement, but both Cornaro and Captain Zeno grabbed my arms. It pained me to see my friend, who had saved me, treated so roughly.

"Tell me who these men are."

One of the guards stepped forward. "These are the two we arrested in the campanile."

"And why were they arrested?"

"Their conduct was disorderly, and we found this." The guard held up the crossbow.

"Does anyone know these men?"

I opened my mouth to speak on Horatio's behalf—

"The large one is a member of my crew," Captain Zeno said before I could get the words out.

"Captain Zeno." Doge Mocenigo turned to face the commander. "Your crew is causing me much difficulty. I suggest you get them in order." He sighed, then motioned towards the prisoners. "Let us hear their stories. You go first." He pointed to Horatio.

The simple mariner's mouth opened and closed but no sound came out. His gaze darted around the room and came to rest on Captain Zeno.

"Go on, man, we don't have all day," Zeno barked.

The direct order had a steadying effect on the sailor. "Yes, captain," he said, nodding his head.

He was an excellent storyteller, and as he related my rescue, the audience was rapt. It was strange to hear my story on the lips of another. I barely recognized it. "Reachin' the shore in a great ship were near impossible. So, I rowed the lad in," he finished.

"And when you reached the shore?"

"The boy took off and I followed him up the bell tower." Horatio gave the guards who held him a foul look, then continued, "When I got up to the top, I saw this cow's behind tryin' to throw the boy off the tower. I attacked."

The crowd, thoroughly invested in the story, gave a cheer and the hair on my arms rose. The doge silenced them with a growl.

"Did you bring a weapon with you?"

"Just these." Horatio held up his fists. The crowd risked another small cheer.

The doge turned his attention to the other captive. "And what brought you to the top of the campanile?"

The man glanced quickly at Foscari, then focused on the floor.

"Your silence convicts you," Doge Mocenigo snapped. "Will you die alone?"

The would-be assassin stood taller. He cleared his throat. "I will not. The man who hired me makes his way to the door this very minute."

Foscari—while all attention was on the doge and the prisoners—was attempting to reach the exit. The crowd closed in, blocking his way.

Foscari's color went from red to white to red again. His countenance crumpled, and his mouth opened.

"No!" he shouted, spittle flying at his words. "I will not have it! It is all lies!" He dove for his wayward footwear and grabbed it. He held the boot up in the air. "This means nothing. This is no proof. How dare anyone question my loyalty? I am the most loyal of Venetians. I am he who cares most for our city. Not these weak leaders and sycophantic noblemen. I care only for the honor and greatness of Venice. Can you not see how you let others overtake us? Our leadership is feeble, making trade deals, painting pictures, bowing and scraping to Rome. Fah! What kind of Empire is this? The Empire of the Sea? We must be the Empire of the World. We must rid ourselves of those who hold us back. Those who refuse to see our chances to be the greatest in all the world. I am he who can take us there. You, you..." He clutched his boot to his chest and raised his finger, pointing at Doge Mocenigo. The pointed finger began to shake. It roved around the room now, desperation leaking out, a vile black oil of deception. "You know this to be true!" Foscari stabbed a finger at each person and they recoiled from him. "You want us to succeed, to be the best, to shine like the sun on this bleak planet. Look at what we have, we can be so much greater, I can make us so much more." His voice was losing its vigor as, one by one, each of the noblemen turned their backs on him.

"No, look at me!" he shrieked again.

But, like a tide, the turning continued, and soon no one faced him.

No one, but me. I did not turn away. I held my gaze fast upon him and saw what his selfish ambition had made him. I saw how his path had gone so very wrong, so twisted by greed and vanity.

I saw.

And I would remember.

CHAPTER 33

After everything that transpired, Nurse Francesca wished to take me to the Pietá and lock me up, but my proper place was with my master, so reluctantly, the nurse returned me to my apprenticeship.

When I returned, Giovanni peppered me with questions, alternately laughing and scoffing at my replies. I did not care for this wealth of attention, and soon seized the opportunity to turn the conversation away from myself.

"What will happen to Lord Foscari now?" I asked.

"The council will examine the evidence to support the accusations against him," he said.

"And if they discover some?"

"His neck will feel the noose," Giovanni said grimly. "Justice in Venice is sure and harsh."

"If they find nothing..." My words trailed off. Neither of the Bellinis answered for a moment.

"It is likely you may be in grave danger," Giovanni said. "Whatever the outcome, you would be wise to watch your back. Foscari's family is of significant influence in the city. They will not take kindly to the maligning of their kin in this fashion, whether or not it is true."

This answer I did not want to hear. But I could not deny the truth in it. My fate now rested in the hands of the council. As thoughts of life as a fugitive from a vengeful family swirled in my head, I was brought up short.

"Stefano!" I blurted.

Both the brothers turned to me with mild curiosity.

"I have somewhere I must be." As the words left my mouth, I jumped up from the table and was out of the door in an instant.

The two called after me, but I paid no heed. It was only late morning; I may not have missed him.

Skidding into the main square, I headed for the Lido. Surely any vessel sailing to Sicily would make its departure from here. I ran along the dock, crying out to the sailors who worked there.

"Which ship departs for Sicily?"

One answered with a grunt and a point. I followed his finger.

It was a small vessel, and they had already pulled the plank up. From my previous sea experience, I judged they were only minutes from departure. Hoisting myself on a nearby flagpole, I shimmied up.

"Stefano," I bellowed like a sea cow. "Stefano!"

The ship creaked and groaned as it began to move. The magnificent beast eased from the dock with a slow, lumbering movement.

My stomach tightened. I was too late. I slid down the pole, getting several splinters in my hands as I did so. Coming to rest on the ground, I stopped as the vessel glided out into the lagoon. My chin trembled as the boat moved away.

"Nico!" The voice came faint on the breeze. I stood up and scanned the deck. There he was, jumping and waving. I joined in, jumping and waving back.

"I am all right," I called. "We did it!"

If he answered, the wind took his words, but he jumped and waved into the distance, and I did the same, never stopping until the last bit of brown disappeared into blue.

CHAPTER 34

Two weeks later, the doge sent for me.

The summons came late in the evening, when the studio was silent and I was finishing up my daily tasks. I was needed once more at the palazzo.

Doge Mocenigo sat upon the platform, his head resting on his hand. There were few councilors present. A quick head count told me the company equaled nine. This must be the famous Council of Ten, the cancer removed from its midst. Though some faces were familiar to me, I could not put names to them all, but some I knew well. I was in a room with the ten most important gentlemen in Venice, from the most influential and powerful families in the Veneto. I bit my bottom lip. My experiences here had always been challenging.

A rustling arose behind me and a warm hand squeezed my arm. Nurse Francesca, all in her customary black, took a place beside me. On the other side, Gentile stepped up.

"Well done, lad," he murmured. Behind me were gathered faces I knew quite well. Captain Zeno, Horatio, Father Vincenzo, and the Bellini family clustered around me, heads nodding, faces smiling.

"Nico." The doge's voice was weary. The last two weeks

weighed heavily upon him. "We meet again. Much has transpired since our previous encounter, most of which you will never know the truth of. But suffice it to say that Foscari will no longer cause you, or anyone, trouble. Today he was sent to the Leads, where he will live out the rest of his short days. However, that is not why I have brought you here. We have called you, and your family," he gestured towards the crowd standing with me, "for one purpose tonight."

He waved to a council member dressed in fine hose and a tight, velvet doublet. The man nodded, looking down at the paper in his hand. "Ser Niccòlo Sebastiano Valiero, it is the pleasure of Doge Mocenigo, the Most Serene Prince of Venice, to thank you for your outstanding service to our state. As an expression of the doge's and Venice's appreciation of your assistance to the great Stato de Mare, your name will be added to the book of nobles. In only a few cases over the last century has the book been opened and altered. This is a rare and solemn occasion."

At this astonishing proclamation, my vision blurred, and a lump grew in my throat. My mouth gaped open and closed like a fish. My heart filled with such joy that my legs trembled under the weight of it, and my body swayed. The hands around me held me up and propelled me forward. As they had done for all my life.

"Nico, you realize the tremendous honor of this moment. Normally, this would be heralded with great fanfare and grandeur, but the circumstances in your case are difficult. We hope that having those who love you here will suffice. We, the worthy Council of Ten and myself, know how you have risked your life for your home. It is citizenry like you holding the future of our city in its hands. It is my wish you receive this honor as a small repayment for your service to us."

"I humbly accept," I stammered, my voice squeaking like a

milk sap. Clearing my throat, I tried anew. "I am moved almost beyond speech, Serene Prince, but whether or not I had received this honor, I would not hesitate to do such again, should it be in my power."

"That is most gratifying to hear, for the truth is I hope to impose upon your service once more."

"My Lord?" My mind clouded as the dankest of canals.

"I need a pupil, whom I can mold and train in the ways of our government, someone of noble character, whose integrity is above reproach."

"By the lion, we lose another good apprentice," Giovanni murmured behind me, and someone shushed him. Nurse Francesca, no doubt.

"Speak, Nico, it is your time now," Fr. Vincenzo whispered.

The room was silent as everyone waited for my answer. The only sound beyond that of my breath was the gentle flutter of the pigeon feathers as the birds roosted for the night amongst the high eaves of the palazzo's attic. The waiting pulled in around me, bearing me up on wings of pure joy.

"You wish me to be your apprentice?" I hardly recognized my own voice. I wanted to pump my fist in the air, to jump like a child at the fair, to shout *hallelujah!*, but I kept my expression relatively calm.

"This is my desire. You realize this does not mean you will one day be doge. The dogeship is a position only the good citizens of Venice can give. But you will learn much and be able to make something of yourself in our magnificent city."

There was truly nowhere else in the world where an orphan of no name could advance from cobbled alleyways to gilded palatial halls. At least, I knew of no other. Would any other state ever ascend to rival the beauty, wonder, and mystery of the great Stato de Mare? I could not imagine it.

CHAPTER
35

It was the next spring before I met Captain Zeno again.

I stood upon the Molo, watching gondolas arrive and depart from the steps leading down to the lagoon. The water lapped against the stone like a hungry dog sniffing at a fresh meal of rabbit. The masts of the great ships rose to the sky, saluting the day.

I waited for one particular vessel to draw near and dock: the Baptista.

As she approached, I noted her proud sides, scratched and dented from the attacks of pirates along the Levant. The stormy season had left her sails worse for their abuse, yet her bearing was still as regal as the proudest queen. I studied the crew who scurried across her top decks. The distant faces of some were recognizable, but none called for my attention.

The gang plank came to rest upon the pier, and several of the mariners dropped to secure the ship on her moorings. I scanned the faces of the arrivals.

"Nico," Captain Zeno called out, his sturdy form striding along the deck above me. "What brings you hence?"

"I come solely to greet my old friend. Word spread through

the palazzo your ship was seen rounding the Lido. How fared you?"

"Well, well indeed. Trade was good. But I have much gladness at seeing you thus, for I have brought with me a treasure which I am sure will interest you."

"Treasure? Is it wise to announce it amid this crowd?" I called back to him.

He responded with a mighty laugh. "I see the time in the society of nobles and councilors has taught you to be cautious of your words. 'Tis well, but in this case, I only mean to allude to a treasure of the heart. I have brought something with me which might be of some interest to you. Attend there. We will descend in a moment."

The ship's company continued in their fury of activity. The crew lowered the sails for eventual repair and dangled cargo precariously by ropes as they hoisted it from the hold and dropped it over the side. The sounds of the sailors cursing and laughing echoed across the whole waterfront. In a few moments, the great captain descended the gangplank. Beside him, a small and somehow familiar figure. The girl had only taken a few steps towards me when my heart jumped into my throat.

As if in a dream, I rushed forward to greet her.

"Nico!" Lisabetta held out her hands. Her dress of peach, gold, and cream brocade swished as she hurried towards me, laughing. The ringing of her merriment cleared my fogged brain. It was the laughter I had spent many hours trying to earn.

"Lisabetta," I gasped, unable to reconcile this composed beauty with the thin beggarly waif I had first encountered in the courts of the sultan some time ago.

"Signorina Sofia Lisabetta di Matteo D'Andrea," Captain Zeno interrupted. "And, it turns out, a cousin of mine."

She laughed again at my foolish and gaping face.

"Oh, Nico, it is all because of you, and My Lady, the queen."

After I recovered from my shock, and the stupidity caused by it, she told the story to rights.

Captain Zeno, on one of his voyages, had chanced to stop over at Cyprus to bring tidings from Venice to the court. On seeing Lisabetta, he had been put in mind of his cousin, Sofia, who had died some years ago in childbirth. Sofia had chosen a man not her equal in her parents' eyes and quitted the family. Her family had mourned her loss and searched for her to welcome her back among them, but to no avail. She had disappeared.

He surmised the little girl could be a relative of his, and after careful questioning of her origins, he kept in mind to search out the truth when he returned to Venice.

"It was with much difficulty I found the wretched serving woman and forced a confession from her. She had been a cook and helper in Sofia's household and had promised to return the baby to her relatives when Sofia knew she would not survive the birth. The wench no doubt intended to make good on her promise, expecting a substantial reward, but as the family had severed ties with their daughter, she could not comply. She kept the child with her, 'out of the kindness of her heart', in her words. But I suspect in the hopes she could turn a profit from the girl."

"Yes, and I suppose I proved most unprofitable," Lisabetta said with a mischievous smile.

"So," Captain Zeno continued, "I returned to Cyprus to bring my cousin home, only to discover the Council had removed Queen Caterina from office."

"Their natural aversion to royalty has been the seed of much discussion over the fate of Cyprus," I agreed, thinking back to some interesting conversations I had been privy to in the closed chambers of the doge. "But Lis—My Lady, what of you?"

"Nico, if you cease to address me as Lisabetta, I will think you no longer consider me a friend. My mistress, Queen Caterina, is promised a property in Asolo. She wishes me to remain in her care, and my family agreed."

"It's not so far away," I said, grinning.

"No, it is not." She dropped her eyes, and a faint pink flushed her cheeks.

"Come, my dear," Captain Zeno interrupted in an over-hearty voice. "We are expected, and I am sure Nico has places to be. Nico, I have some maps and things for Doge Mocenigo. Will you ensure he gets them?"

I nodded, taking several packages he held out to me. "Certainly. Captain, I hope to join you at sea soon; some experience on a sailing vessel outside of the hold would serve me well."

"Wonderful, wonderful!" He clapped me on the back. "I should like to have dinner with you tonight, Niccolò." Taking Lisabetta's arm, the two headed together across the piazza.

"Wait," I cried, jumping forward, stumbling as I moved. "When will I see you again Lisabetta?" My voice cracked.

Lisabetta met my anxious question with an impish smile, looking up at me through her long eyelashes.

"You are having dinner tonight with the captain; perhaps I will be there." She turned back, clasping her cousin's arm, and floated down the piazza.

I remained with my gaze on them until they were out of sight. My pulse raced with a strange quickness.

With my free hand, I reached into my pocket and pulled out a familiar coin. Flipping it in the air, I sauntered across the Piazza San Marco towards the palace. As I reached the far side,

I noticed a small lad, shifting from one foot to the other, eyeing the coin as it rose and descended.

"Here," I said, tossing it to him. He caught it deftly, a lad who was good with his hands.

"Thank you, Ser," he said, eyes big.

"Use it well. If you take only what is rightfully yours, it is blessed and will prosper you much." I smiled and mounted the steps to the palazzo.

As I joined my footsteps with the countless throngs who had roamed this tiled expanse for centuries, I saw afresh the real Venice.

Venice, alone in the world, served her people. Venice was like a living jewel, germinating from the unlikely seed of swamp and sea. Cracked here, chipped there, but covered with a fine patina. She burgeoned, despite the flooded streets, despite ungodly forces pressing at her door, despite the avarice of men.

The bells rang out from the campanile, their resonating sound signaling the end of the workday. Shopkeepers collected their wares, moving them back into their stores, shuttering their windows and locking doors. This ritual had gone on for generations and would, I knew, go on for generations more.

Had I saved the city? I could not say.

But if it had not been me, Venice would have raised up another, for Venice was necessary, and her fate rested in the hands of God.

Glossary of Terms

Basilica: A church designated at a special location by the pope of the Catholic Church. There are four major basilicas and many minor basilicas around the world. Basilica San Marco in Venice is a minor basilica and believed by the faithful to house the remains of St. Mark, whom it is named after.

Bocche dei Leoni: Italian for Lion's Mouth, also known as the Mouths of Truth. These were Venice's version of a complaint box. Elaborate faces carved into a wall—often lion's faces—with mouths that served as slots into which Venetians could slip notes accusing government officials and public figures of wrongdoing. Precedence was given to signed notes, but all were read and given serious consideration. Accusers were severely punished if their claims proved false. The earliest recorded occurrence was in 1618, well after Nico's time, but I snuck them into my story anyway. When Napoleon invaded Venice, he had them removed, but six remain hidden around the city to this day.

Bucintoro: The State boat of the doge. This boat was rebuilt frequently, so the style changed, but there was usually a small terrace on the back where the doge would stand to throw out the ring into the sea at the ceremony of the marriage of Venice to the sea.

Campanile: an Italian bell tower. The Campanile San Marco was first built in the 12th century. It was rebuilt several times, most recently after a collapse in 1902. The tower is 99 meters (325') tall and has a statue of the Angel Gabriel on top.

It's unlikely that there was a bell in Nico's time, as they principally used it as a lighthouse, but that's the great thing about writing fiction, you can change things to suit your story. Records show the belfry was likely added in the 16th century, not too much time after Nico's story takes place.

Campo: a small square in an Italian city.

Corno: The doge's ceremonial headgear.

Council of Ten: Ten members of the larger ruling council who were selected to act as judges. It was these men who would meet in secret to discuss the cases of the accused and decide on their fate.

Doge: The dogeship of Venice lasted for one thousand years. The doge ruled for life, but unlike kings and queens, the doge was elected from the elite families of Venice. By Nico's time, the doge was considered a prince, but he was subject to the laws of the land. He could not do whatever he wanted. The word doge comes from the Latin *dux* which means leader.

Festa Della Sensa: The Festival of the Marriage of Venice to the Sea was a time to celebrate the city's relationship to the water. Started over a thousand years ago, the festival continues today. The highlight is a rowing competition in St. Mark's Basin, a much-anticipated event.

Osteria: Italian for a small restaurant or bar.

Palazzo: Italian for palace.

Piazza: A large square in a town or city.

Piazzetta: A small square in a town or city.

Procurator: In Venice, the procurator was in charge of the Basilica San Marco. It was an honored position which came with power and respect. Typically, the procurator would have been responsible for the function of the orphan hospital where Nurse Francesca worked, and Nico stayed.

Sala del Maggiore Consiglio: The room in the Ducal Palace where the Great Council would meet.

Scuole: Groups of people banded together to see to common interests. Similar to medieval trade guilds, but they did not necessarily have to belong to the same occupation.

Ser: Term of respect for Venetian gentleman, like master or sir.

Stato De Mare: A term used to describe Venice, the Empire of the Sea.

Soldo: A coin. Plural is soldi.

Acknowledgments

I would like to thank anyone and everyone who supported my long and winding writer's journey in any way. You know who you are. I send a special thank you to my best-writer-friend-forever Paris Gibson, who's insight, encouragement and loyalty to my work has kept me going all these years, and to Mary Dunn who's love of writing inspired me to keep on going. Also, to my writer's group, Writer's Ink: Moy Ahmed, Jeff Schill, J. Mercer, Jenn Van Haaften, Karla Manternach and Vikki Menuge, you made this book infinitely better than I ever could on my own.

Thank you to the efficient and encouraging team at Immortal Works for loving my book and giving me this chance.

The biggest thank you goes to my wonderful husband, Doug, without whom this would never have happened, and to my ever-encouraging kids, Rebecca, Nicola and Christopher who never, ever, ever stopped believing that I could do this. You all mean the world to me.

Lastly to the beautiful city of Venice that inspired me, and countless other artists, dreamers, philosophers and poets to strive to be unique and lovely in a world that needs more of that.

ABOUT THE AUTHOR

Nancy grew up in a little family, in a small town on the outskirts of a bigger city. Besides her family, the two things she loved most in the world were reading and playing pretend. When she grew up, reading was allowed but playing pretend was sometimes frowned upon. Since that was the case, she now writes books so that the stories running around in her head still get a chance to be real. In between writing stories, marrying her college sweetheart, and moving to a new country, she had her own little family, and settled in another small town on the way outskirts of a much bigger city. Some things never change. Find Nancy on twitter @nancyemc, Instagram nancyemcc66, Facebook and on her website www.nancymcconnell.com.

This has been an
Immortal Production